YOU & ME

ALSO BY PADGETT POWELL

Edisto

A Woman Named Drown

Typical

Edisto Revisited

Aliens of Affection

Mrs. Hollingsworth's Men

The Interrogative Mood

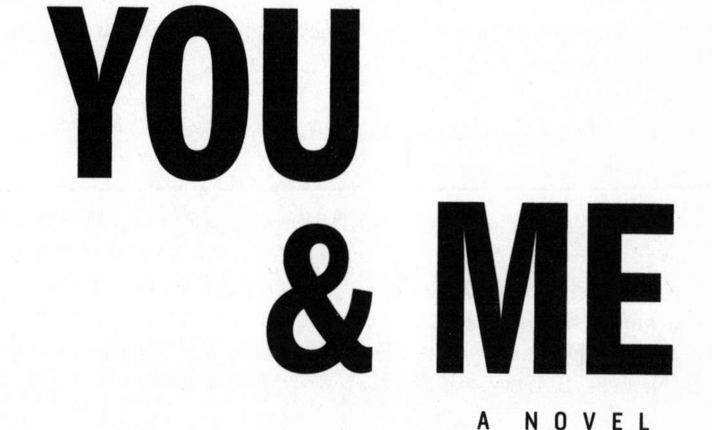

YOU & ME

A NOVEL

PADGETT POWELL

AN IMPRINT OF HARPERCOLLINS*PUBLISHERS*

First published as *You + I* in 2011 by Serpent's Tail, an imprint of Profile Books Ltd, London.

Portions of this book appeared in *Harper's, Little Star, McSweeney's, Subtropics,* and *Unsaid,* and on NarrativeMagazine.com.

HarperCollins books may be purchased for educational, business, or sales promotional use. For information please write: Special Markets Department, HarperCollins Publishers, 10 East 53rd Street, New York, NY 10022.

FIRST U.S. EDITION

Designed by Suet Yee Chong

Library of Congress Cataloging-in-Publication Data

Powell, Padgett.
You & me : a novel / by Padgett Powell. — 1st ed.
p. cm.
ISBN 978-0-06-212613-9
1. Beckett, Samuel, 1906–1989. En attendant Godot.—Parodies, imitations, etc. 2. Middle-aged men—Fiction. 3. Experimental fiction. I. Title. II. Title: You and me.
PS3566.O8328Y68 2012
813'.54—dc23

2012009520

12 13 14 15 16 OV/RRD 10 9 8 7 6 5 4 3 2 1

for Amanda Dahl

who loved forty-four

Do you know where you are, Mr. Barthelme?
In the antechamber to heaven.
—from *Hiding Man: A Biography of Donald Barthelme*
by Tracy Daugherty

He felt rather like someone lying in a bath after all the water has run out, witless, almost dead.
—Malcom Lowry, *Under the Volcano*

YOU
& ME

Somewhere between Bakersfield, California, and Jacksonville, Florida—we think spiritually nearer the former and geographically nearer the latter—two weirdly agreeable dudes are on a porch in a not upscale neighborhood, apparently within walking distance of a liquor store, talking a lot. It's all they have. Things disturb them. Some things do not.

&

There's about fourteen ounces of this left.

There's a hair in it.

It's okay.

If you said "lard-and-hair sandwich" to her, my mother would gag.

Was that a Depression food?

I think it was a joke, but I'm not sure.

I've heard of butter and sugar sandwiches. But that would hardly be a Depression meal.

I have no idea what the Depression was, or what the war was, or the wars after that, or before—I don't know anything at all, you get right down to it.

So these codgers have something on us.

Yes they do. That is our cross to bear. Everyone knows shit but us.

Let's make the best of it.

Fuck these codgers.

They come over here with that shit, tell 'em to go eat a lard-and-hair sandwich.

I will.

&

I wish something would *move* out there.

Where?

Out there. On the broad plain of life.

I *thought* that's where you meant. Me too.

Be nice, some action.

Of some import.

We could say we did something . . .

With ourself.

Telling a codger who says quite properly we ain't doing shit to eat a lard-and-hair sandwich does not in the long term constitute a life.

No it does not.

Well if a war doesn't break out on you, and you don't stumble into making money, and you can't play ball, and women treat you wrong, or men, and you aren't a movie star, and you don't have any talent, and you aren't smart, etc., what are you, we, supposed to do, exactly?

Live until we die, without any more pondering than a dog, is my guess.

And that is a good guess, but it seems less a guess than the natural conclusion every hapless human being comes to on his witless own. It's a default position. It supports all dufus behavior.

Yes, it even supports "the pursuit of happiness."

Indeed it does.

&

Today we are becalmed, as we are daily becalmed.

Every day we are becalmed.

Becalmed is our middle name.

My uncle was named Jake Becalmed. His brother was Hansford Becalmed. Their brother was Cuthbert Becalmed.

No one is named Cuthbert Becalmed.

Wait. The fourth brother was Studio Becalmed.

No mother names a son Studio.

This one did.

Is it Italian?

What?

The name *Studio.*

We aren't Italian, is all I can say to that.

So this kid is called Studio, and what happens to him?

Well he was killed in the war.

I mean what happened to him as a result of his name.

Nothing.

Nobody razzed his ass.

No.

He was Studio, end of chapter.

As far as I know.

Studio Becalmed.

No, their name was not really Becalmed.

That was a joke.

Of sorts.

We aren't very funny, when we joke.

No. Because we are becalmed.

Studio. I like him.

I do too.

&

Studio Becalmed had one great affair before his brief life was terminated, with the actress Jayne Mansfield.

Who herself was not long-lived.

Indeed not—beheaded on the Chef Menteur—

Yes, in the days when stars went overland in cars instead of in airplanes as they now do.

Anyway, when Studio frolicked with Jayne Mansfield he was like a tiny man lost in the Alps.

I suspect that that is a vulgar reference to her giant bosom?

It is if we let it be. On the other hand what do we know of Studio and his inclinations? He may well have been spiritually lost, not in mountains of flesh as it were but in the blond glow of happiness, or something.

We are safer assuming ourselves vulgar, and maybe Studio too. After all, he was to die in World War II, and men wanting breasts then or otherwise desirous of flesh were not to be discredited as they are today.

Healthy desires today are all clotted up into Healthy Choice.

Yes, and the smart man chooses Not Wanting if he wants to be safe.

Studio, let us say, was the last healthy man.

Why not? I am certain that he was. He was healthy and then he was dead, and Jayne missed him, then died herself, as much of a broken heart as of decapitation.

It's a lovely conceit. Studio lay in the mud, Jayne in the untopped car, forever sundered, or forever together if you can participate in the large fiction of their frolicking together in the final Alps of Heaven.

That is a wonderful phrase. I would propose we name us a dog that.

What? Alp?

No. Final Alps of Heaven. They use long names in registry, you know.

I knew that. What would we call the dog?

I think *Final* would be amusing. *Of* would be not bad. *Alp* is out.

Agreed. *Heaven* would require explanations unto the tedious.

We could say we inherited the dog from Studio Becalmed and Jayne Mansfield, that we are the godfathers to their child.

Fifty years after the fact.

Yes.

This has promise. Tell these codgers, Don't pet Final Alps of Heaven, you asshole, that is the dog of Studio Becalmed and Jayne Mansfield, even you will recall the mountainous breasts she had, *hands off!*

When they look at us as they will, we say, Even if you were gay we would not let you pet that dog. If you were gay of course you would show some respect for that dog. We are having fresh basil pesto for dinner, will you stay?

I bet they won't.

Of course they won't.

Beanie weenies and let them cornhole the dog, they'd stay.

Oh don't be uncharitable. Beanie weenies and we let them play with the dog and they'd stay.

Yes, you are right.

I am always right.

True. Does it get tiring?

Be real. Of course not. Why would it?

It's supposed to.

Yes, and I respect you for playing the straight fool, but really, Constant Rectitude is one of the large peaks in the Final Alps of Heaven.

Let us get another dog and call him that, use his full registered name. Or you could even adapt the name for yourself. Con, Connie, Rex, Tude, Constant Rectitude!

Constant Rectitude, go to your room until your father gets here with his *belt*.

Constant Rectitude took another hiding today for his constant transgressions.

Constant Rectitude and Studio Becalmed have run away to join the circus, but they joined the Army instead in error and will die as patriots rather than as syphilitic roustabouts.

Failure is to success as water is to land.

This is the great secular truth.

I believe I will speak this great secular truth to the meddling cocksucking codgers when they come over here telling us we are not shit, rather than get into what kind of sandwich they might eat.

The sandwich advice is too much of a mouthful all around. And Don't pet the dog may not convey the nuance and force we want.

We have failed, yessir, because water is pandemic. Is that too subtle?

Not for me, probably for them.

Fuck them. Are they not the party to whom I am speaking, whom I seek to impress with my meaning and get them off our back and stop begging us for sugary food and stop petting our inherited dog from a man dead fifty years who skied with his nose down the ramp of Mansfield's Alps—are they not whom I seek to have comprehend me and thereby desist in their presuming upon us? Well then fuck them, I will not be clear merely because being clear is my object.

Well put. As well put as any failed man ever put it.

Thank you. Thank you, Constant Rectitude. I would be obliged were I to be henceforth known as Inherent Muddle. These are our new Indian names. I saw two arguably better ones in Poplar, North Dakota, just off the Fort Peck Reservation. They were Kills Twice and . . .

And?

I have forgotten the other name. Also Something Twice, but it was something mundane, not killing, something even faintly ignoble, like Sleeps Twice. I can't recall it.

Failure is to success as water is to land.

I should have written down the names. I was sure I would remember them. They were likable Indians, I presume, those brothers Kills and Forgets Twice or whoever they were.

If we had better *names,* we would be better men, is what we seem to have arrived at.

I'll not argue with that, nor do I know a sane man who would.

When the fucking codgers come over here, just ask them who the hell they are, and when they say their names, just snort!

Snort like a hog inhaling a new potato!

Snort like an armadillo reading a newspaper!

Snort like a man gasping for air in the Alps!

If that school bus goes by here any slower, I'd say it's prowling looking for houses to break in to.

Codger at the wheel?

Codger at every wheel on earth.

&

I forget where we are.

Me too. I too. What do you mean, exactly?

We are over here, I see that, and all that is over there, and this over hereness and that over thereness is a small part of infinite other relations of hereness and thereness, I see all this, but then I get a bit forgetty, and, just, don't have this particular-in-aggregate setup in my head, and I say something like "I forget where we are." Then I recover, regain my purchase on the system of therenesses, and see the finite hereness of us, but of course by now I realize I have no idea where any of this is, where we are, what we are doing, what we are, in the large picture that makes an aggregate of all the particular systems—

Just shut up.

The driver of that school bus is prowling the streets looking for a stray child to molest. He has the perfect cover. Almost any child on earth will voluntarily enter that bus if the door opens and the monster sweetly proffers a ride.

What is your point?

Was there a time before this, say when Studio Becalmed went to the war, when a school bus itself did not represent the moral depravity of the world?

You had like the Lindbergh baby did you not?

Isn't that different?

I suppose. Why are we now so feckless when we were once arguably heroic, just two generations ago, do you mean?

Precisely what I mean. Two generations ago we would go out there, yank that codger out of that bus, give him a good beating that did not actually put him in the hospital but which decidedly ran him out of town, our object, and the matter would be handled, no legal repercussions, no perverse crimes on our watch, no counseling services involved, no law, nothing but bluebirds and rocks and sticks and good picnics and war when necessary and good heavy phones and not too many of them.

Mayberry.

Yes.

It cannot have been so easy. We are suffering some kind of distortion, I feel certain.

I don't argue that. But do you not agree that we should go out there and beat that pervert off that bus, and that we won't, and that if we won't we submit to the prevailing illness that is here now, whether or not it was there then?

Yes, I agree.

Then Q. E. effing D.

Are we going to be okay?

No. No, we are not.

Okay.

How many of us are there?

There's the two of us, right now. You and me. You and I.

Right now, still all two of us—

Right, we have not become less than two, yet. Still two people here, not yet disintegrated into less than two, although we are arguably indistinct from another, so that the proposition that there are two of us may be limited to a kind of biological truth. Truth is not the word I want . . .

I get your meaning, Kemosabe.

The two of us indistinct from each other, in the here here not altogether distinct from the there there, but we are two of us here and okay so far.

But shaky.

Yes, shaky.

Okay. What I want to know is, you know that controversy over butter versus margarine, what I want to know is how did they ever purport to sell something they elected to call *oleomargarine*? Can you tell me the etiology of a word like that, and even if it is a scientifically honest word why would they not have changed it for palatability as it were? Like a movie star's name? Did you know that the fighter Jersey Joe Walcott, for example, was really named Raymond Cream? Rocky Marciano versus Raymond Cream. Don't put butter on that, here use this oleomargarine. Fix you right up. You are going to have great difficulty tonight with Mr. Cream, Mr. Marciano.

I can't help you with any of this which troubles you. I have my own problems.

Another thing bothering me: what is the song involving a Mr. Bluebird sitting on one's shoulder? I like that song. I can't recover enough of it for it to be of any comfort, but I like it, or think I like it, if there is in fact a song with a Mr. Bluebird witting on one's shoulder.

Did you say, "witting on one's shoulder"?

I meant sitting.

You might have said shitting.

Yes, but I said witting. It's a new song, I like it. I want a bluebird witting on my shoulder.

Don't we all. Imparting the wisdom we lack.

Our problems will soon be over, when this bluebird alights.

&

I don't think we should go down there anymore across that little stream, over that . . . what is that, a vacant lot, for sale? and then by that store—is it ever open? *was* it ever open?—or by that school, across that impossible highway, looking into those seedy houses there, that one with the girl in it all the time, where are her parents or is her parent or at least her dog for God's sake? and then just wander back home as we do . . . I don't think we ought to keep doing that. I can't say why. I get this feeling after we've done that trip that we are boys, it is the kind of route boys would make, pleased by the nothingness of it, the slim opportunity for some probably criminal event to offer itself to them or upon them, you have to admit if we were to encounter anyone on that trip it would be poor folk, it could not be else, and they would fuck with us if we were boys, but since we are not, more precisely since we don't see them anyway, they don't, I don't know, I just don't think we should take that walk anymore. We should go see famous cathedrals and art. Don't you think so?

I do think so.

Because that girl in that house reminds me of once talking a girl into showing me the goods in her playhouse, all very genteel you understand, a cute playhouse with proper cardboard appliances in it behind her proper suburban home, a lovely affair really until one day during the goods display she flinched and looked out the window and I asked what was it, and she said, "Nothing, but my father told me not to do this anymore," and I bolted, end of affair, I not knowing that was a father's job in this context and not knowing that it did not include persecuting me, I did not want the fellow after me and most certainly I did not want him knocking on the door of my house and involving my own father, not knowing my own father's job would have been to smile and promise to handle it and secretly approving to have gently dissuaded me from any more affections unto Kathy Porter because she was not, apparently, to be trusted—knowing nothing, I ran from the playhouse, not stopping as per usual to climb the long rope swing into the live oak which had been my end of the bargain, Kathy's reward for exposing the goods: she got to watch me make this heroic climb into the mossy ether and become a little Tarzan to her Jane by sliding back down the rope, hands and legs and loins on fire from the titillation in the playhouse and the friction of the exhausted fall, the most agreeable fall. There I'd be tumescent in the dirt, which Kathy knew nothing about and I was only starting to know something about. It is for these reasons that I no longer wish to walk in that neighborhood and see that poor girl alone in that ratty house and wonder what is to become of her.

I am in full sympathy with you, as much as I will miss looking at the little creek, and pointing out as I must that there is not a famous cathedral within five thousand miles of us, or ten.

What is it about the little creek?

Its forlornness, its slightly iridescent stagnation, its unsupport of anything alive that one can see, its dubious mission, its helplessness, its pity, its bravery, the miracle of it withal in even remaining *wet*—

Which sometimes it does not—

—Exactly.

You see in the creek *us*.

Yes I think I do.

It is our mirror.

It is.

Well let us not be so vain.

All right. We shall cease going to the creek.

Our hair is also not good but I do not see that we can stop it. Our hair is us but we must have it. We are not good and we must admit it.

I think we do a fair job of that. As good a job as might be asked of anyone.

I hope that you are right.

Will it matter, in the end, if we have been good, done well, etc.? Whence the very idea that it will have mattered?

Whence the very idea of *good*?

Yes, you playhouse playboy, you nine-year-old Tarzan, who came up with the idea of goodness?

It is one for the sages.

&

Do you ever feel you've left your heart in San Francisco?

Yes, all the time.

Not there of course but—

Of course not there, but yes, this is what we have done, left it somewhere.

Or did we perhaps not really have a heart, and have come to know it?

This is perfectly tenable.

Do you think hand-wringing now will effect a recovery?

No.

We shall regard our absent hearts as total losses, regardless of whether we had them once and lost them or never had them at all?

This is the prudent course, I think.

I'm with you, then. Is wanting to go see the creek or not go see the stupid anemic ditch we have to call a creek in trashed-out suburban America part of this losing of the heart and not knowing whether it is a loss or a congenital absence?

I think it is related, somehow.

Okay then. The issue is settled.

We could do with some ice cream though. Makes the boy-man feel good, heart or no.

It's a cold, brutally unhealthy comfort.

The very best, most honest comfort.

Ice cream is like maggots in a field wound.

Tell that to the codgers.

It would stop them for a moment in that calm stream of strong silent knowingness they so gallantly ride.

Those codgers get you worked up.

I am a cat to their dogging. I admit it. I am delicate and vulnerable and I must inflate and arch and spit or they will have me. I admit it. Mine is the weak strength of bluster.

You are a good man nonetheless, in our tribe of weaklings.

Thank you. To say that requires of you a heart, which you have momentarily retrieved from San Francisco. I see steam on the mountains across the way.

We have mountains across the way?

We do now. They flowed in overnight.

I did not know we were on a fluid landscape.

To my knowledge we are not, there is no such thing, yet there are mountains with clouds strafing them gently, looking cottony and kind and the mountains inviting not looming or threatening as big ones might look. No Everestage, I mean. These are junior mountains, with trees on them, big hills properly speaking I suppose, I am most innocent of mountain terminology and taxonomy.

The clouds are moving across them, prettily, as if on the way to San Francisco. Folks' hearts are in those clouds.

Godspeed.

I am tired today.

We are tired every day, are we not?

We are. But one can suddenly tire of tiring, and move down a quantum level.

Let's get to absolute zero and see what happens.

This we may be doing, if we perceive the land out the window to be flowing. Your poor little girl's shack may have been whumped into the next county by a mountain, the distressed creek now a noble rushing cold cataract of clear and gurgling and clean strength. Running over smooth rocks, harboring sturdy fish, appealing to bears.

It's too much to hope for. I am going to bed. Rompoid Sturgeon.

What?

Nothing.

&

Where exactly *are* we?

A very good question, requiring care in the answer. Geographically we have no idea. In the geography that has no place, that which obtains when the there is not there, can you dig it, we are between Jacksonville, Florida, and Bakersfield, California. I have never been to Bakersfield so I will tell you that I imagine chain-link fences in strident disrepair, all manner of paper and plastic blown into these fences, the asphalt and concrete expanses they once purported to contain crumbling and earthquake-looking, a scree of rubble and grit blowing about as if on the floor of a pizza oven the size of Baghdad, if you will excuse me an excess, a glare that signals white heat, anyone you run into want to beat you up, for money or for sport, and no way that anyone like Frank Gifford is ever going to come from there again, if he ever really did, and even the kind of indigents in country-western songs about it are noble compared to the riffraff coursing through its collapsed streets now. And now we go downhill to Jacksonville.

That's where we get the girl in the shack and the piddly creek that disturbs you so much.

Yes. That creek. It has that orange shit in its shallows that is not shit but that conveys every impression of sewage that can be conveyed. It looks like rusted cotton. There is not outright mud but dirty sand. Not outright water but enough to support seven minnows, two crayfish, one mud turtle, one giant water bug, half a leopard frog, a third of a garter snake passing through, and no water bird but a flyover by a depressed songbird just keepin' on keepin' on, trying to find a concrete birdbath for a decent drink. Add a rubber or a Fritos bag, maybe a purse, and you about have it. Pair of panties. This is where we are.

You shouldn't have to feel the way you feel.

No, I should not. But have you ever heard of *feeling* insurance?

The premiums would be impossible, the actuarial tables a nightmare.

And this is why Lloyds does not offer it. Blues insurance. Quite an idea.

Verification tricky. Who would *not* claim?

Precisely.

Let's go down to the creek and stare Despair down.

All right. Fortify ourselves with some Kool-Aid? Chocolate milk? Morphine? Lip balm? A Dr. Bronner's peppermint shower? Sit-ups? Read this article about adult-retardation hospitals being phased out of existence by progress? Put on clean underwear? Promise ourselves a shoe-shopping trip after the creek stroll?

You are incoherent, almost.

The edge of incoherence is a strong position, militarily speaking. Not incoherence outright, but the selvage as it were, affords a bidirectional moment between dissolution and precipitation, liquid and solid, that can absorb about any assault, any direction, gross or subtle, acid, base, land, sea, or air. The mind properly speaking is in a condition suggesting pickle relish, or chow-chow as it gets called. I am in chow-chow readiness for the creek. Head full of chow-chow I could go on and watch you watch the girl in the shack and not be over disturbed.

You don't get disturbed there. You did not climb the rope with Kathy Porter's parts in your fetid brain and a hawser burning through your crotch as the earth spun to meet you and drive your weakened knees into your chin. The true difficulty of such a maneuver is of course avoiding the terminus on the end of the rope, board or large knot. That is why you have to clear away from the rope. Getting away from a rope as you slide down one is a subtle athletic proposition, because of course as you get free of it, it is weightless and can offer no resistance to your push, so you are pushing an object that affords variable, decreasing resistance, and if you push it too hard once your weight is clearing it you will introduce into it a curve that will wave down the rope and whip the end of the rope, which is what your push is designed to enable you to avoid, into approximately your genitals by towing your buttocks through them. Thus you can see why I could no longer afford to perform this trick for Kathy Porter once she had informed her father of our inclinations in the playhouse. I could never have successfully negotiated the rope escape had I had to worry also about him staring down at me once I hit the ground in my tumescent exhaustion from the climb and fall. Can you imagine the difficulty of sticking a landing for Bela Karolyi if you'd been diddling his daughter?

You hadn't been diddling Mr. Porter's daughter had you?

No. I had not touched her. I did not know that was part of the plan. I just wanted a look. But since I did not know about touching, I thought looking contained the entire crime. Having looked was enough if I had been lying in the dirt under their giant live oak with giant Mr. Porter looming over me, and small meek Kathy standing by regarding her two heroes in the throes of some contest—fighting over her, were we? It could have been an interesting moment, but I at least was not man enough for it.

But today we are men enough to walk into the slums of Bakersfield and look at a poor girl in a shack.

Well, yes. It is different. The voyeurism here involves her poverty and our hopelessness. That is to say, she is truly hopeless, and we are only constitutionally hopeless, as men who cannot connect to the world of men proper, and we want something from her, from her true and honest despair as opposed to our bogus and self-generated despair.

I had no idea going to the creek could offer this much.

Kathy was apple-cheeked and freckled and hopeful, willing to entertain me in my excitement and not outright condemn me for it, even after her father gave her the finger wag. This other girl is dull in the eye. You have seen her. We have no communication with her. No one in her community is going to approach her with a proposition as innocent as mine to Kathy. That is the little moment that transfixes me when I see her. How good to Kathy I was, fumbling in the early teeth of desire, how good her father was to us both. How this girl today has none of that goodness. How the world has rotted in fifty years, is what I am saying.

There was a poor girl fifty years ago in the same way.

That might be true, but I was not there to see her. Somehow today I am. Something has changed which effects that simple, or not simple, change.

You are today a dirty old man, is part of it.

That is why I am taking a Dr. Bronner's peppermint shower before I go out winderpeekin'.

&

I once heard Peter Jennings say "passenger manifesto."

He was referring to what they said as they went down.

He was clever then.

Yes.

He was a man of the world, in the world—

And we are not.

Precisely.

How did this happen, he get to say "passenger manifesto" and be a national icon, if not some kind of oracle, at least a grand national-news-anchor corporate mouth, and we are nothing?

Hoyle and Darwin, and lard-and-hair sandwich. Peter Jennings never teased his mother with lard-and-hair sandwich, and you never would have said passenger manifesto, and there you have it.

Thank you for wrapping up another conundrum of our times.

De rien.

I would certainly like to have some ice cream.

&

What are these things here?

I've never seen them before. Is it things or one thing? Where was it?

On the porch.

Let's get out of here before they or it explodes.

I am terribly becalmed by a washing machine. Is everybody?

Not everybody, surely, but most.

Had I the affluence of Peter Jennings I would put a dedicated sleep washer next to my bed, just run a low-water light cycle, no pollutants.

You could always toss in, say, your underwear at the last minute, the clothes you discarded before bed. To be practical.

You could. You could transfer them to the dryer if you got up in the night, and put poppin'-fresh BVDs on in the morning. Change your whole outlook on life, the sleep washer.

You could connect it to the bed itself and get a vibration quotient. The dryer heat could be used to toast the bed in winter.

Man. This puts a whole new spin on "white noise."

But we don't have the affluence of Peter Jennings. A washing machine is not a frivolous appliance for us. We would not survive were we to say "passenger manifesto" on national TV. We would be subject to the cruelest of ridicule, dismissal, were we momentarily so irregularly lucky to have been employed in the first place.

So we best resign ourselves to imagining Peter Jennings sleeping next to his dedicated washing machine, his bed gently shaken, gently toasted, snapping into his fresh panties at the top o' the morning for another day of lucrative suit mouth. Just resign yourself. He delivers the manifesto, you're the passenger.

I'm too depressed to go to the creek now. Looking at the girl is utterly beyond me.

Let's just sit here.

Let's.

She'll understand.

She too is a passenger.

Bakersfield is a passenger of place.

Without a manifesto.

We are without a manifesto, not on the manifest.

Let us just sit here.

Yes.

&

In the grove of trees down there is a table and a barber pole. You place your hat on the pole, and—

I do?

One does.

Why?

Would you allow me to tell you?

Prosecute your voyage.

One places his hat on the pole and a barber will emerge from the woods and give one a haircut. It is an old barber who has cut the hair of certain famous deceased men. Now he is enfeebled and shaking so badly that you will need repair to another barber for corrective attention to your new and sad-looking do.

Is the barber pole turning?

Yes. Why?

Because I would feel odd, if not outright dizzy, watching my hat turn while waiting at a table in a grove of trees for an old barber to emerge and give me a bad haircut.

I do not mean to suggest you must do it.

No no, of course I will do it. It is a grove of trees with a table and a pole and a haircut to be had, I will of course do it. Something that is done is *to be* done, period, in the interest of good and modest citizenry.

In the interest of being a good fellow, you mean.

That is what I mean.

Yes, well, then the barber of some famous dead will affect to cut your hair as you sit at the table in a pleasant breeze by a table in the shade of the trees. The whirling of your hat will not disturb you overmuch once you begin to worry about the undeft motions of the man with scissors and razor about your neck and throat and eyes and ears and nose. The straight razor under the nose when the nose is pinched up—the razor poised for the Hitler cut, that cut which will take out the hair which would otherwise form the Hitler mustache, I mean to say—will be your worst moment.

I will sail through it as if it is the Fifth of May. The table—is the table perhaps early American, unlevel, of two or three broad virgin boards badly joined?

You have the picture, my friend.

I do. I will enter the grove of trees, placing my hat on the pole, sit in the straight-backed chair, await the geezer, accept my scary butchering, in the corner of my eye my fedora turning dizzily, my arm resting on the uneven planks of pine or walnut or cherry since indeed it could be real wood if what you say about the table is true, all of this in the shade of the trees and in a breeze. I will be oddly and momentarily a complete man living a full life.

&

I don't want to go down there. Something could eat me—us. I forget you're here sometimes. Something could eat us.

I don't regard that as the worst way to go. No matter how it went down, you'd not waste away. If the thing was large enough to attack, we might presume it large enough to get it over with. You'd be part of an appetite, part of Life.

No old-folks home for you, eh? Down the hatch!

That is right. Laugh as you will.

I worry about *small* things eating me—malaria is worse than grizzlies.

Of that no doubt. I am not going down there either if you think there are mosquitoes.

Let's stay right here in our nets and eat bonbons and get fatter and whiter and stupider and lazier and more cautious as we have less to be custodial of.

Pustulent academics!

I have never heard that word before. Is it a word?

Pustulent? What other adjective could derive from *pustule*?

It sounds good, I grant you. But the red vapor of Air Spell Check puffs from your mouth when you say it. I see *pestilent* and *postulant,* but no *pustulent.* You look momentarily like a sloppy vampire when you say it.

I wish I could be a sloppy vampire. My life has come to naught.

Don't start. Let's not go there. We live there, so let's not go home.

That phrase, "go there," is funny I think because it approximates an abstract translation of the English idea behind it.

What are you talking about?

An Italian would say, "I have large friendship and I like to go there all the time." If you put the move on a Frenchwoman who was not ready for it, she might say, "Don't go there," and stop your hand.

I see.

These bonbons are hard as rocks.

They came from the little Filipino lad you purchased that brutal haircut for.

He chose the barber.

No, the barber is his uncle, and he had to go to him once you made it so public you were funding the venture.

Is it my fault the uncle is inept? They'd have known the child got his hair cut no matter how it was financed. He looked like one of those faux primitives.

Now he looks like he suffered a head trauma at Sunday school.

He looks like a houseboy.

He may, but he is bringing candy to us that might be ten years old.

Well, we are free to lie here and complain of it, so what is there to complain about?

A fattening man may not bark?

I think not. Not honorably.

Do we still pretend to honor?

We do.

All right, then. I say no more about the granite nougat from the wounded boy. I will say that when I came into the café you should not have humiliated me that way.

What way?

"Are you not wearing panties?"

Oh, that.

Yes, that.

It did look as if you'd forgone pants. Everyone in there agreed. That is why they laughed.

They laughed because I gave them that Dietrich pose.

Well, that too. But the pose supported the notion that you had no pants on under that beach shirt with those tails.

These people don't know what to make of us now.

So let them not know. You become wooden in your old age.

Who does? Them? *They?*

No—*you.*

&

Because we don't have to do anything unless we want to.

Are you done with that?

With what?

That sentence?

Yeah, why?

Because it's not a sentence, and it's inane, for starters.

Who hung you up in the stirrup?

Did what?

Twist your drawers.

I am too tired to deal with you.

Me too you.

You too me. You sound like Tarzan.

You Jane. What the monkey name? They had them a chimp didn't they?

Cheetah.

They had a cat name Chimp?

Prolley did. They was stylin' jungle folk.

I remember when Tarzan take a shower in his clothes in New York City and rip out of his wet shirt with a muscle show.

A muscle show?

He stretch like, like a cat, and his like Arrow single-needle-tailoring oxford shirt rip to shreds right there in the shower.

Did that turn Jane on?

You know it did. Jane in her leather skirt.

Do we not have anything else we could think about?

We must, but I can't think of it.

We should read a book, about the atom bomb or something.

Or about the philosophy of aesthetics.

Or about explorers, or history, some political and economic history, this is what we should be talking about instead of Tarzan and Jane stylin' jungle porno folk with a big monkey named for a big cat.

Did Tarzan do any vine swingin' in New York?

You know he musta have, acause how else could he get around except when he was riding elephants—

—and that time he run on foot to stop Boy from going over the waterfall on the giant lily pad—

—yeah, he run then, but allus elsetimes he swingin' everywhere, and what I want to know is how did they, you know, get him the vine equivalencies in New York, like what—steel cables and shit? Tarzan could just happen on some loose electrical wire and swing to a new building.

Oh man you know he could, he was a dude.

For example, we should be discussing like the differences between Hellenistic or even Roman conquerors and Central Asian conquerors, I am thinking largely of Timur here and the path of centuries-old degradation he legacied by virtue of the policies of razing, whereas say Alexander preserved, Caesar preserved . . .

And so you have Europe as opposed to Uzbekistan, this is your thesis?

Yes it is. Do you think Johnny Weissmuller was a steroid user?

Did they have them then? He was in the Olympics in 1924?

The idea of steroids before the rise of Hitler is strange.

Steroids is what the Nazis were all about. Bullies kicking sand in the face of six million ninety-pound weaklings on the beach.

That shit is hard to believe.

Yes it is but is it not the only thing that explains the US of A going into Iraq "unprovoked"? Isn't the cordata of that game the presence of Israel and the shadow of them steroids?

You are a wise man. Is it possible to get Tarzan movies at Blockbuster?

You will recall that Jesse Whatwashisname irked the Nazis in the 1936 Olympics running faster than the bullies.

Owens. We are I think confusing Weissmuller's Olympics with Owens's. They couldn't have been in the same games, could they?

Yes. My point is that today if they redid Tarzan, Tarzan would be played not by Weissmuller but by Owens. Or Denzel as Owens.

No, it would have to be Owens, because if subs were allowed then Schwarzenegger would be Weissmuller.

Ooo. That sounds nasty.

That is nasty. Do you know how to get mold out of a car? I am afraid I enclosed a car under a car cover and now it looks like an orange been in the basket two months, an olive velvet interior head to toe.

You car messed up. I guess you could put fifty-five gallons of vinegar in it and drive around.

We could go down to Blockbuster in the vinegar and get Tarzan.

&

It is not for me to say.

To say what?

Anything.

Then why announce that you've nothing to say?

It's just a polite filler, like the little business at the end of a newspaper column.

I see.

No you don't.

You're right, I don't.

So why say you see when you don't see?

All right. There's nothing for me to say either.

But we keep talking.

Yes.

We must.

Must we?

Apparently. Evidently. I love *evidently* used that way.

Remember that hurricane victim sitting inside her collapsed house saying, "Evidently I'm in shock."

Evidently she was.

Evidently.

It is hard to say what she thought she meant. The evidence that she might be in shock did not seem wanting.

So she meant, "Obviously I'm in shock"? "Apparently I'm in shock"?

No, she meant, "I'm in shock," but some force made her preface it with "evidently." Evidently my house is destroyed and I am therefore in shock.

Well, you know, let's say she was in shock, and the evidence of that fact might be, to her, obscure. Say she has heard about shock, and is feeling strange, with her house gone, but she is not wailing or gnashing, she's numb, and she gets the idea that she would be wailing and should be wailing and if she's not then maybe she's in shock. There's some evidence that she's in shock, evidently.

So the old bird is actually pretty smart, not inane?

It is not for me to say.

&

Are we perfect?

No.

You have such a poor attitude.

I confess it.

You would.

Should I deny that I have a poor attitude?

Anyone with a proper attitude would deny that he has a poor attitude.

But I have a poor attitude because I confess that we are not perfect. I should claim that we are perfect, indicating that I am a lunatic.

No, indicating that you are a positive thinker.

You would like me to be more positive?

Yes.

That will make it all better?

Yes.

All right. We are perfect. Tomorrow we will make a million dollars. My dog will never die. The dead one did not die. No more deer will be struck by cars. My intellectual fundament is not subject to measurement or decline. My soul is eternal. The hungry children of the world tomorrow will find bacon and eggs in their stockings. Rosy human potential is limitless.

See? Is that so hard?

No. It is not hard at all. Imbecility is the greatest feel-good power on earth. It's why so many are drawn to it, like religion. It is a religion.

There you go again, taking a turn for the worse.

I must pull up out of the trees. I recant. Imbecility is a rare affliction that we are rapidly eliminating as we evolve into the perfect species on the happy planet. Any more talk out of me of the other sort and I'll just wear the dunce cap for a bit.

&

I'm bopping in my head to *something something the Midnight Rider.*

What?

It's a song. I never listen so I only know the last words in a line, if that. *Something, something, the Midnight Riiiider . . .*

Why don't they saponify hemp oil itself?

Who?

Well, they, They, anybody, but this Dr. Bronner outfit would be a more logical party than say Colgate-Palmolive. They recently made a big deal of putting hemp oil in place of jojoba oil in their soaps.

The famous hippie soaps.

Yes. Hemp for the hippie, you see.

Does the hippie want hemp in everything he uses?

That would seem to be the premise. So what I am saying is why not just take straight hemp oil and saponify it?

Maybe it would be lousy soap.

It probably would be lousy soap, but what's that got to do with anything? Hemp oil is probably a lousy additive compared to jojoba oil, which itself was regarded as a magical elixir and selling aid for years. Now it's out. Hemp is in. I'm seeing this. When the hemp soap is worn down to suppository size, you slip it up the bombay winking portal *like* a suppository and get high.

Or you cut it down, like a plug of chew—

Or they just *make* it in suppository form, like these little parlor soaps in baskets in B&Bs—

Those are called parlor soaps?

I don't know. Novelty soaps? Demitasse?

They have wrappers on them, *pleated* wrappers—

Like candy, sort of. Anyway, the hippies just pop these hemp-soap suppositories in and go about their buzzy days.

The oil surely won't deliver a buzz.

I'm thinking it won't, but that won't be a total dissuasion. A man can have an assful of gushy hemp oil on hand anytime a narc elects to conduct a body search. It will be a kind of counter-cultural chaw. The laxative value is probably high.

They can sell it as Soap *Not* On A Rope.

This is my million-dollar idea for today.

&

These bullet things—

You mean our heads?

Yes, we have to do something about these bullet things, our heads if you insist—

What can we do about our own heads?

I don't know but we cannot very well sit around uncomplaining and content with powder for brains, can we?

From an ethical point of view, or from perhaps a social point of view, you are right, we do not want to be perceived as having been content to having had bullets for brains. But from let us say a naturalistic point of view, is one really capable of repudiating his own brain? Has this been done too often in the animal kingdom?

So you maintain we just sit around like the howitzer heads we are until we go off?

Yes, we just calmly take aim at an enemy downrange, which is anyone who happens to be downrange, and sooner or later, according to high principles of military art or acknowledging the low principles of happy circumstance putting a victim in our crosshairs, we kill. We use our heads and annihilate. It's easy. It's what we are designed to do. We are bullet heads. You need to relax.

That much is true. I do. Need to relax.

We all do.

All us bullet heads need to chill.

Right on. We could hurt our*selves* if we don't.

Bullets don't just go off by themselves.

No, they don't.

Exhale.

Okay.

They've started letting us take the yoga classes if we wrap our heads in towels.

That is good news.

Yes it is.

&

That is a man with fifty functional rain hats.

What do he paw fink?

What?

A man with fifty hats makes me think of a joke about a bear. A country boy is told that a bear hibernates all winter. What do he do? the boy asks. He sucks his paw, the teacher says. What do he paw fink? the boy asks. You needed to have been there.

Where?

I will estimate that I heard my aunt tell this about 1962 in a rented cabin on the Crooked River in Georgia. Boozists and card players.

Big hit, was it?

Medium hit. They lost a large quantity of beer leaving it in a chest freezer too long, looked like ropes of intestines and brown glass in there. Good snake count outside. Rough river with some salt water in it. Nice place. These places are all gone now. At least I fink they are.

I fink so too. My paw is dead.

Mine too. This is one reason why I do not discredit totally a man with fifty rain hats.

I am not following you, but I dig where you comin' from.

My paw could wear one of those hats were he here. I did not really know him. That is a shame. Had I to do it over again, and if he himself had fifty rain hats, I would not laugh at him for that, is all I am—

—Yes yes, perfectly clear.

You going to pay me, or whut?

How much you worth?

Four grand.

Four grand.

Yes.

Okay.

You don't think I am worth four grand?

I said I'd pay.

You said, Okay. You have doubts.

Okay, I doubt that you are worth four grand.

Okay. Pay me.

That is what I said I would do. No one who argues to effect the initial status quo is worth four grand.

I made an error. I have mental problems.

I would say that you do. It may take your four grand to begin to address them.

That would be a waste of money. My first purchase will be a deep-fried hamburger, followed by a nice leather bag for some new toiletries. I lost all my toiletries in the misplaced-car incident, or series of misadventures related to losing the car, I should say.

Your toiletries.

My toothbrush and chiefly my Eveready badger-bristle shaving brush, which I had had over twenty-five years. It's like losing a child, or a parent. When I get a good new ditty bag and a shaving brush in it I can begin to reassimilate into normal living.

Hat, boots, beer come next. Redhead on my arm. Hot-air-balloon vacation, that kind of thing, snap me back into my BVDs just fine.

Four grand will get you there?

I should think so. Yes.

You'll stop this trebly warbling and trembly walking around and all the goddamn moping and incoherent expressions of your *pain* as if only you have any, and the incessant holding of your large face in your tiny hands?

Yes, I shall stop all that.

Four grand is cheap if it will stop the lugubrious flood of you.

Well, pay up, and I'm a new me, that's all I can tell you.

&

Is it better to have continuity of no content or discontinuous content?

What is “content”?

I use it as an irritatingly vague substitute for seriousness of purpose or meaningfulness in living, or something similarly perhaps as irritating as “content”—

I get the drift. I would say it is better to have content without the continuity if the alternative is smooth unbroken vapidness such as the sort we practice in these dialogues every day.

I'll mark you down in the intellectual column. I am not surprised. I'm penciling you in right beside Bertrand Russell.

I'll take it. One might be penciled in beside, say, Jerry Lewis.

Listen, I'd rather not talk today. I want to go watch old tennis players be displaced by young tennis players and the crowd weep as they retire and then start cheering for the new cocky-bastard upstarts who have sent them to pasture. This I want to do today, and nothing else. I want a cool soda water in my hand and a hat on my head and to not be overweight myself watching the elderly depart. I can from this position think gently of my own death.

You almost got some content going on.

I got it going on.

You'll look like a tennis groupie but you'll have secret ponderment.

No one will know.

You'll be a subversive in the stands, a thought arsonist. You'll be like a Frenchman.

&

I'd like to see some flying dogs.

Are there flying dogs?

Not that I know of. Seeing some would improve my mood tremendously, though.

I suspect it would. Mine too.

Cheer us right up, flying dogs.

Raining cats and dogs.

Like to see cats bouncing off cars.

Why'd they call combat air battles "dogfights"?

They wanted to see flying dogs too.

&

And today, today what shall we do? What we shall do today is . . .

Is carry placards on the street.

For whom? For what cause?

I do not know that. May we not just carry a generic placard for A GOOD CAUSE? Let people fill in the specifics, according to their own designs and divinations of what cause needs supporting?

They might arguably be much more likely to actually support the cause if we let them supply it.

Indeed they might.

So how does our sign read? Here, I have the fat Sharpie, the white board, these handy furring strips.

What are furring strips exactly?

These sticks.

I know it's those sticks, but why are they called furring strips? What is *furring*?

Can't you just make a sign and put it on a stick and go out on the street with it and start a movement and change the world without pestering the shit out of people about a word?

You can say "furring strip" without a clue what you are saying and be unbothered?

Write STAMP OUT FURRING—THE MORAL IMPERATIVE OF OUR TIME on your placard. On mine I am going to merely put

SUPPORT THE MORAL IMPERATIVE OF OUR TIME. This covers the spread. Let's go.

Let's take some of that lemonade. It'll be hot.

You got it. Stamp out sugar, the moral imperative of our time.

You is a Communist. You put that on your sign and we are both dead men.

&

The red Ban Lon shirt and the dark walnut clubs made the strange deformed Negro boy wielding them look remarkable.

That is the most idiotic utterance I have ever heard come out of you.

Why?

Why?

Yes, why?

Because if the combination of Ban Lon and walnut and deformity moves you only to remark, as the word *remarkable* suggests, then you suffer a catastrophic failure of the imagination.

I do. I do suffer that. So do you. Are you mental?

I thought you said *arf* you mental.

You neglect to note Negro when you list Ban Lon and walnut and deformity.

It is a spectacle beyond the mere remarkable if a boy, white or black, is in Ban Lon with walnut clubs and deformed, to my mind.

The remarkable knows no color, in the progressive view.

Yes. Are you meaning to specify, by the way, a walnut clubhead or clubs with walnut shafts, because I think that—wooden shafts—is even more . . .

Remarkable?

Yes. Certainly by that I would mean also more visually striking and more anachronistically arresting. One would ignore the white or black crippled boy in fey spongelike material to focus on the antiques in his possession. One might even worry that he would break them, if you specified that this boy is actually golfing.

Actually he is not. He is sitting on the hood of a new BMW with a Swedish-looking model of tremendous height and minimal clothing posing for photographs for an automobile advertisement. Insofar as I could gather. For all I know, now that I think about it, they may have been advertising her clothes, or his, conceivably they were advertising the girl for a men's magazine, though it did not appear a lascivious endeavor.

&

I think I want me some morphine.

Why?

Because I 'magine it is good.

You have not had it?

No, not the real thing. I want to sleep in that red field outside of green Oz, with Dorothy. Or without Dorothy. The prospect of sleeping with Judy Garland is not halcyon.

The prospect of sleeping with anyone is not precisely halcyon.

Right. That I can forego. Were it not for the stupefying nuclear force of hormones the race would cease. I just want the morphine—a wide calm sound in my brain, my body itself as smooth and cool as water. An heavenly balm. All my cells whispering kindly to me, "Everything is all right." This I want.

You want so little. You are filled with jejune longing, for an old man.

Jejune Longing is the chewing gum of Life. It's what they named Juicy Fruit after.

&

Isn't the essential question whether one reuses split shot or not? Doesn't that just about say it all?

Don't you think it's configured a bit narrowly? What if, say, one doesn't fish?

All right. Let's explain that a split shot is a tiny ball of lead with a split in it which allows it to be crimped onto a fishing line for the purpose of sinking the line. And that usually once a split shot is crimped onto a line and used it is thrown away if it has not been already lost in the course of the fishing. But that a certain kind of person will take a crimped split shot and reopen it, usually by pressing a knife into the original crimp and gently reopening the shot, being careful not to go too far and cut the little shot entirely in half. And that this certain kind of person will take pleasure in this salvage beyond the saving of two cents or ten cents or the effort of buying a new pack of split shot that much sooner. He or she will take pleasure in this microsaving of a tiny lead hinge that is not a micro pleasure but instead some kind of huge and hugely gratifying anal balm.

Have you lost your mind?

Well, yes. And of course that is what we are talking about, don't go getting Pat Boone on me now. The question that this split shot question asks is whether a man has lost his mind and does not care, or whether he has proudly arrived at the terminus of his adult life, or at the prime phase of it as it bears unto the sunset, with his "sanity" in hand. If he says, "I don't save split shot," we know he is correct and adult and proud and all grown up, as it were. If he says, "I save every split shot I can," we know he is just as proudly crazy and that he has refused to grow up.

And we think that he has actually a superior position in this refusal.

Yes. He would not then also say, for example, "I support our troops."

That would be one dimension but there are many dimensions to this lunacy that is not lunacy, you mean.

Yes, I do so mean.

I wish that you were a woman sometimes.

I do too. That you were.

Because we could make love instead of talking all the time.

Yes.

We could make love as it is, but . . .

I just can't see it. I like the political dimension of it, the nose-thumbing, but God, the actual thought of it . . .

Why don't we find us some split-shot-saving women?

It would be better if we found some who would not themselves save split shot but who would humor us in our saving split shot. I would really like to have a girl who would hold open the little Take a Boy Fishing Today tin while I carefully pressed the knife into a used split shot and then let me put it safely in the tin, looking briefly to see if you can tell the difference between the used and the virgin split shot, and then say to me, "Come to bed, sugar, them split shot are safe and sound." Wouldn't that be grand?

I think that would be the best thing in the world. Since "It Opens with Two Fingers" she could slide the tin shut with two fingers! You could be a perfect idiot with a girl who wanted you in bed.

And with the perfectly preserved little lead hinge! That is really what the split-shot question seeks to discover: Are you a perfect idiot or are you some kind of custodial correct adult ass? Isn't that the idea?

Yes. That is the idea.

&

I wake up trepid. Do you wake up trepid?

I fear I do. What does *trepanning* mean? Maybe I wake up trepanning. I wake up trepanning if it means shaking from trepidation.

Are we but recently afraid, or were we always afraid but too slow or blustery or full of hormones to know it?

We have always been afraid. We are only now sufficiently feeble to visibly shake. We quaked all along but were steadied by testosterone and received bravura. We looked fine.

We stood firm.

We shouted, *"Hello! Stand and deliver!"* If it were a man before us, we said, *"Cross me and I will kill you!"* If it were a woman, we said, *"Take off your clothes!"*

Now we jump off the trail and hide in the woods if anyone approaches.

Lest a woman say unto us, "Cross me and I will kill you," or a man, "Take off your clothes."

What goes around comes around—is that not the way it is popularly put these days?

I believe so. You may also say that the chickens have come home to roost, frequently said by people with no knowledge whatsoever of chickens, when chickens do not leave home to begin with. It is apt for their enemies to say upon the assassinations of John F. Kennedy and Martin Luther King, for examples, that the chickens have come home to roost, and no one will question the utterance.

Such people are people not yet trepid. We should not be uncharitable with them. They will come in time to tremble and shut up.

Out the window I not infrequently see chipmunks.

A chipmunk is professionally trepid all its life.

A chipmunk is a cute and honest poor soul that does not presume.

&

What do you know about the desert?

Nothing.

Okay. End of subject.

Should we go?

Yes. We should go.

To revel in our not knowingness.

To be put off by the desert because we do not understand its desertness and are frightened by it and disgusted by our not knowingness.

But then is it not the case that after we are frightened and disgusted we will fall under the illusion that we have learned something about the desert and be less unhappy with it?

Yes. Our tiny growing familiarity alone, as we sit there or walk around parched and frightened, will convince us we now know more than we did before the onset of the fear and the disgust, and we will feel better about the desert.

Veterans of an hour in the desert, we will like it, a little bit.

Yes. When you see a Gila monster emerge like a bizarre beaded purse you will love him as if he is your own mother. You will imprint on him as does a gosling on the first thing that it sees move and you will have a mother and not be sore afraid as you were even though they say your mother can kill you if you let her chew on you.

Or a sidewinder! I was born to love a sidewinder. Do you remember Studio Becalmed?

I will never not remember Studio Becalmed.

Nor I.

What is your point?

I believe that Studio Becalmed had a sidewinder in his pants.

That is vulgar and senseless and juvenile and almost funny. God, in His infinite wisdom, has seen to it that our mothers do not chew on us when we are infants but wait until we are older and can take it.

Or at least can resist it and issue poisons of our own.

What if Studio Becalmed in the Final Alps of Heaven repudiated Jayne Mansfield and took up with Jejune Longing?

It disturbs me to think of that, even if by that point Jayne is headless, as I suppose she would be, even in the final alps of heaven.

You don't think that things would be restored to some kind of corporeal pristinity in heaven, or perhaps be noncorporeal?

I cannot say. If things are noncorporeal will it be meaningful that Studio "repudiates" one woman for another? Do we not mean by saying "repudiate" that he would eschew Jayne and lie down with Jejune Longing? In your view will there be no intercourse in heaven? Is it worth going then?

You have a point. Somehow I do not see rutting and grunting in heaven. Nor can I see it allowed exactly in hell. This very prospect is somewhat like the desert to us. Will rutting and grunting be allowed in the afterlife?

What would happen in heaven were Studio to say, "Jayne, be okay if Jejune Longing came over?" and Jayne were to say, "Sure, babe"?

A sidewinder touches the ground with only ten percent of himself, if that. He does not get burnt and he does not bog down in all that sand.

He knows the desert.

He knows no fear and no disgust.

Do you ever have a longing for a good, fast car?

Sometimes. I like the restored hot rod.

I saw a man on television presented with the surprise gift of his junk car fully restored. He wept before it. The mechanics who did the work laughed, gratified and sympathetic, to see this man weep before his new hot rod. All he could say was, "It's everything," and sniffle. He opened the hood and beheld the specialness under there and fell back in a whole new paroxysm of ecstasy.

He's an idiot. I envy him.

I regard him a larger idiot than you do and I envy him more.

He is a kind of sidewinder, is he not?

Well, that seems a bit of a stretch, metaphorically, but I will call the weeping idiot we admire a sidewinder if you will. What harm could lie in that?

I am particularly drawn to advanced technology in sparkplug wires and to the arresting colors they now make them in. They are not black now. They are orange, chartreuse.

Wires the color of liquor!

People the color of dogs!

Why did you say that?

I don't know.

&

In what environments should a man have it together? In a chamber of surgery, with a scalpel in his hand?

Yes. There he should have it together in the extreme.

Are there other venues where he should really have it together?

No. Let us say he is holding on to the back of a garbage truck and stepping off it as cans of garbage on the curb are approached and swinging these cans of garbage into the truck and setting them down empty, or tossing them any old way, and stepping back on the truck (which has not come to a real stop) as it progresses toward the hundreds or thousands of cans remaining on the route—he does not need to have it together for this, and this is essentially not unlike any other human endeavor on earth just now, except for surgery.

By "just now" do I detect that you believe that at one time more men had it together?

You do detect that suspicion. I cannot call it a full-on belief. I just think that given the near total dissolution upon us now that it, our dissolution, could not have ever been greater, not even when we were crawling from the cave, and that to have survived this far we must have had it together more back then than now. People did not always eat sugar and talk all day on cell phones and go to war simply because they were told they were unpatriotic if they did not.

I am not unsympathetic to your position. I wonder though if the case may not be made that people would have always eaten sugar and talked on cell phones had they had access, and that what has alarmed you is the novel *number* of idiots now upon us. The base percentage of crackpottage remains the same but the absolute numbers have shot through the roof. For example: you can wrestle yourself to the ground weighing solicitations for you to contribute funds either to save an endangered paucity of animals or to feed an endangering surplus of starving people, who are the primary endangerment to the animals, but nowhere does anyone solicit funds from you to limit the numbers of the starving people.

That's an example, exactly, of what?

I don't know. I do not have it together well enough to have any idea.

I thought so.

Here's another example: I heard recently of a bear eating cherries off a suburban cherry tree, who, the bear, then killed the tree.

And this news serves us how?

It serves my thesis: In earlier times the bear never would have wrecked the tree. A bear is no less survival-savvy than a man, and is as smart, etc., as anyone who has ever seen one ride a bike in the circus without killing everyone concerned can attest. Were this bear not subject to the same forces that have made men the trivial fat loose cannons they are today, he would never have harmed the tree that feeds him. He is a symbol of modern man in modern times.

He'll eat anything?

He'll *do* anything.

I myself am frequently visited by an odd vision which is possibly not germane to whatever you are talking about. I see myself drinking tepid and not very satisfying water from a tangerine-colored aluminum tumbler in extreme ambient heat, I see a water moccasin, and I hear the noise of cicadas or some other leg-sawing racket-specializing insects in pine trees, or at least in the bush all about, a noise that rises and falls in volume and possibly pitch in a way that seems to resonate with my very head at moments, or within my head, I don't know precisely how one speaks of resonance but think I grasp it, physically speaking. It is possible that this noise even gets the rather yellowy orange tumbler I am drinking the hot water from to vibrating in a way that shocks my teeth and makes the water taste bitter. The water moccasin is a benign, sturdy, calm presence in all this, not, as it were, holding his ears or calling for ice water. The water moccasin alone, I now realize, *has it together*.

It *is* germane to whatever I am talking about.

It would appear to be.

That surprises me.

Me too.

I did not think even what I was talking about was germane.

To what?

Well, to anything at all in general and specifically to what I was talking about.

Can one talk about something and have it be not germane to *itself*?

Well, yes, I think this may be the quintessence of not having it together.

Talk that is not germane to its intention—in other words, the nattering of the mad.

Yes, if the mad have an intention.

They probably do. They have just lost it.

I wonder if your water moccasin would allow himself be petted?

I could put my hand inside the otherwise useless metal tumbler and stroke his neck and find out. My sense is that he would not mind.

Can you, in your vision, be careful so that he cannot get a bite in above the tumbler on your wrist?

Yes. I will present him the bottom of the tumbler, slowly, right to his chin, and stroke him under the chin if he assents.

The caterwauling bug song will abate as you do this.

I will momentarily not hear it. The sound will be there but I will have pushed the "attenuate" button. I have seen one of these on a fancy car radio. My mind will be with the mind of the moccasin.

You will forget the bad tangy water and the stupid metal cup and the bug song.

I will be somewhere else.

&

Will we be *able* to cross the river and rest in the shade of the trees, is what I am wondering.

You mean as opposed to wondering if we should, or if it will occur to us to want to do that, or—

No, I mean, precisely, Will we be able to cross a river and rest in the shade of the trees. I grant that we are too daft to have it occur to us. Perhaps you have not noticed, but the river is a concrete ditch now, usually, if it is not altogether underground beneath roads, and the trees are an automobile dealership. A man would need say today, after his arm is blown off, Let us cross that water-control canal there and repel the salesmen and crawl under the F-150s, where I wish to die.

We are living when before we would not have lived, and now we are dying where we would not have died.

That is almost epitaphic. When he should have not, he lived. Where he should have not, he died.

It will perplex the cemetery goer.

The cemetery goer, in my experience, is already perplexed. I see no harm in keeping him that way. I need some coffee, my friend.

I am in want of recreational drugs, untattered clothes, psychological counsel, carnal affection, a dog, and a child upon which to lavish trinkets and advice.

I fear for this child.

Not more than I.

&

What is Life like once it fully collapses around you, sir?

Has it fully collapsed around me?

You were averring this last night after your thimble of wine.

My thimble of wine has made my head hurt.

I refilled it for you several times, imprudently. At your insistence.

I insist on nothing anymore. I don't have it in me to insist.

That's what you say, sir. But after a thimble you will insist on another.

I dispute it, and it is not in me anymore to dispute, either.

You said, "My trumpet of vino is exhausted, Charles, fill it quick because Life has collapsed around me. Julia Child is dead. Fill it before I join her." I felt unable not to comply with this request, sir, as you had phrased it and supported it.

The ghost of Julia Child is a powerful force.

Yes. You once used the ghost of Crazy Horse to similar effect.

I think of them together. Julia cooks prodigiously, drinks, accepts photographers. Crazy Horse sups succinctly, plans military campaigns, eschews photographers. They both die. Life has collapsed.

I can't continue to pretend to be your manservant. Or catamite.

It challenges me too.

You addressed me as "Charles."

I was thinking of Ray Charles, who has also died and contributed directly to the collapse of Life as we thought we knew it.

You pour a little wine for me tonight.

Will do.

&

Have you noticed . . .

Have I noticed . . . what?

I am certain that you have noticed. I was pausing because of that certainty. I was relocating the emphasis to my question. Have you noticed, any time lately, the phenomenon by which when you meet someone whose personality you object to that your own personality is shifted to a counterpersonality, as it were, to which you also object, arguably more than you object to the offending personality of the other?

Is the classic instance of this when you visit your parents and are thrown into the ghosts and contours of yourself when you were, say, a teenager and in full combat against their lunatic officialdom?

That might be the classic instance of this phenomenon, yes. But I think there are more frightening instances of it. I met a man recently who came on like a car salesman when there was no commerce between us and it put me into a guard, an almost Royalist snootiness that I very much did not like. What I did not like about it, beyond being made into a false personality, a boor, was that I could see he was oblivious to it, to my being a snob, because he was continuing on his program of taking advantage of me, or of the world in general, of which I just at that moment must have appeared to be a part of in front of him.

What put you off about this fellow?

He was smiling effusively and kept repeating my name. He was positioning me to like him by affecting to regard me as special. It put me into the role of a loan officer, or a hawk sitting a branch watching a mouse on the ground, or an off-duty prison warden.

Nothing wrong with the off-duty prison warden.

Come to think of it, you are right.

You should thank the man.

I've been ungenerous.

As usual.

Yes. You're no Christian, Senator. I knew Christian.

&

Rosy turtles. With green eyes and yellow hair.

Yes?

I see them.

Hair?

Yellow hair.

Does it seem strange, hair on turtles?

No. Some of them are cropped short, like tennis balls, some spiked-out and gelled-looking, some just look like boys with yellow hair. Or girls.

So it's unnatural-looking hair?

Well, it does look bleachy, but I think that is a conclusion we draw faced with yellow hair, on turtles or no, and in this case, for some reason, I am inclined to think this bright yellow hair is natural.

Custer was said to have—

Famously. Custer was a boorish happy ass. These turtles, my friend, are serious and somber, responsible . . . citizens. I nearly said dudes.

Where are these turtles?

In my mind. In the province of my mind.

Is there any kind of natural surround for them or are they—

They are just there, turtles, without props or context; nor do they weirdly float about or appear deliberately isolated. When you see turtles with hair, with agreeable expressions, rather friendly-looking dudes, you don't examine the area around them overmuch, I find.

A reasonable position, with hairy turtles in view. No prob from me here. I need to get out, get a little air, purchase a small quantity of sugar from a vendor, snack on it as I idly perambulate, whiling away what little remains of my little and inconsequential life, of my dear dearth of time on this hallowed planet.

I am sorry I have set you off. With my turtles.

Not at all. I feel just excellent. I am fond of your turtles and live vicariously through them and have a sunny disposition for your having seen them. These visions sustain us. They are all we have.

Amen.

They make us religious, almost.

&

What is the big picture?

Please. Don't.

Don't what?

Start. I can't. Today. No more big-picture mauning. Your yellow-haired turtles is a big-picture maun at an acceptably veiled, small-picture scale. That I can take.

You have invented this word, *maun*.

Maybe I have.

What does it mean?

I can't take that either. You're asking me things you know. You know what it means.

I suppose. Studio Becalmed mauned, then he met Jayne, she died, and he mauned some more, differently from before, and when your dog dies you maun a little. And so forth.

It's a rather warm-soup and somewhat philosophical kind of longing. Studio was not free of mauning even when he knew Jayne, of course.

Of course. I was speaking hastily and sloppily, of course.

There is no pressure upon us not to be sloppy.

But there is pressure that we not be *too* sloppy, lest we not strike the happy-accident monkey keys and say something that pleases us.

Do you think often, or ever, of Miles Davis doing all that

dope and blowing into his horn until something flies out that pleases him and everyone around for miles and miles?

That is why they called him Miles.

If we are not too sloppy they will call us Inches.

&

Why do we talk?

Why would we not?

I suspect that is why we talk: what would we do if we did not talk?

Precious little else, darlin'.

My point.

Your point is that we do nothing but talk . . .

And that if we cease, we do nothing, are nothing.

Well, given how little we talk about, we are next to nothing already.

I dispute you not.

You brought this up, suggesting you might dispute it—I'm sorry, here I am talking inaccurately, doing the next-to-nothing thing we do sloppily. I mean to say: your bringing this up might suggest you are concerned with how little or nothing we are.

No, I am content to be nothing. It might be argued, for example, that a secretary of defense talks about matters that are far from the nothing end of the gravity-in-talk spectrum. I would rather we talk as we do than as secretaries of defense.

We are not con men, whatever else we are or are not.

And if we are, we con but our own self, and we have occasion to think of things to say that we don't say, and think even of, say—I do this, I don't know about you—I think once in a while, say, of the stray dog Jesus, wending His handsome way, turning down girls.

I see Jesus in his mind alone take the T-shirt off a nubile with his teeth and shake that shirt as a dog does a rag.

Shake the life out of it!

Shake it, Jesus buddyro!

Does the girl stand there admiring Him?

She stands there with her arms crossed modestly over her desert-chilled chest, smiling enigmatically, patient with the Savior in His paroxysm, saying to herself, I'll never tell, I'll never tell . . .

Oh! Don't you long for the days when discretion reigned?

I long for the days when it existed at all.

Do you prefer to fish from the bank or from a boat?

I prefer to fish from wherever fish are less likely to be taken. I am fond of the fishing show on television.

Is this too a quiet vision of Jesus?

It is probably something of the sort, yes.

Could you dig a Flood?

You mean another big one?

Yes.

Yes. I'm in. Two of everything on the boat, the rest of us die. I am *in*.

&

There are some people who should die before the Flood.

Who?

Well, all these regimes that make refugees of millions of their own people, these regimes that bomb other countries to set them free, these gangs in Toyota trucks gunning down barefoot people, of course they all need to drop off right now. Just crumple over into the mass graves they have prepared for someone else. Then there are some others I want to see gone.

Are you talking about the phone virus?

I am. A person talking on a cell phone in his car, when he switches off the car, crumples over on the seat right there, just like a regime war criminal. Anyone dumping trash not at a dump gets the virus and crumples over on top of the crap he dumped; he will be found there by the sheriff if not by buzzards first.

People that throw shit out of a moving car chap my ass as much.

And mine. When so much as a plastic wrapper goes out of that car the perp will vomit prodigiously into his own car, and when he pulls over to address the issue and switches the car off, *phitt!* For that matter a person walking who tosses a paper cup to the ground will go down on his knees and have about five seconds to contemplate the cup before he too joins the unrighteous dead and improves the world that awaits the Flood.

&

What if we called the Salvation Army and had them come over here and clean us out?

Like, strip the joint?

Take everything here except us and what we're sitting on.

What would be the point of this?

I am not sure.

Do you have any relatives living?

I must. Somewhere.

Me too.

Are you essentially alone?

Yes. It's you and me. You and I.

God.

Tell *me*. Does this relate to having the Salvation Army come over and take our shit?

I think so. I have a vision of our sitting here, rather nattily somehow, in a clean place unbothered by biographical detritus and other riprap.

I love that word. After the Salvation Army comes and rescues us, though, we cannot make a cup of tea, or sleep well.

This is true. Maybe there is something wrong with my vision, technically. But . . . holistically—is that really a word?—I think I am onto something. If we could sit in these chairs unperturbed while everything was taken and have nothing then around us but the air we breathe and a thought or two, and our monkey chitchat, we would somehow be very superior.

I think you are having a monastery vision.

Maybe I am. I am a monast, or want to be. May one say that? Or is it monk?

Totally out of my ken, monking and all its affairs.

I heard a child once counting to one hundred to prove that she could, and when she said "forty-four" she stopped herself and said, "I *love* forty-four!" and then resumed counting. It was funny, and only a child could have done it, and only once. It was a unique moment in that child's life, and in mine.

Are you going to cry?

I might.

Go ahead. Don't call the Salvation Army while you are blubbering. And don't be blubbering after they come and take our shit.

Of course not. We'll need a stiff upper lip after that.

Mr. and Mr. Stiff Upper Lip sat in their chairs stoically as the Army of Salvation invaded their home and made natty and uncomplaining monks of them. The bums who toted their belongings past them could smell the fine cognac in their snifters.

That is a fine vision—you've put a Degas touch on my original pedestrian idea. I'd call the Army right now if it did not require my finding the phone book. Do you think if I called 911 they would refer me to the Salvation Army?

You could tell them you need emergency salvation and see.

Is it possible that we do have some cognac?

Not.

That's the funniest thing kids have come up with in forty

years. Before that it was the Jim Thorpe thing, I guess. It was similar, syntactically.

Man, there was a horse.

Apparently.

Cowboy up. Let's go to the liquor bunker and get cognac and evade the angry brothers and get back here and be damned glad we have chairs to sit in and beds to lie on and toothbrushes to perfect our smiles with, and like that. I am not ready to sit for Degas yet.

&

A dark thing.

A dark thing what?

I had a vision of a dark thing—

A dream?

No, not a dream, just a sense of something dark, a dark place or effect, an ominousness . . .

And?

And I can't develop it. The nearest equivalent I can think of is that alleged cold space said to obtain in haunted houses. It had that, but it wasn't overtly paranormal or threatening or weird; it was just a sense of some muted thunder under a place or a time, a set of emotions that was like a dark curtain, ever so slightly foreboding. I thought I was going to be able to get up and seize it and make literal sense out of it, you know, a set of objects terminating in sensory experience, but I can't.

Are you quoting Trouser Snake?

Indeed I did.

Don't. Anymore.

Okay.

Quote Studio Becalmed or quote no one.

Studio, bless his short mortal soul, did not say enough for us to ferret out quotes. He was, after all, Studio Becalmed, not Studio Blather. I don't think Studio could have ever been troubled by a "vision of something dark" that he couldn't put his finger on.

No. In our mythology of Studio, he went fishing or walked around in the woods and then saw Jayne one day and romped thereafter in the Alps of Heaven, dead or alive. He was not given to analysis of figments of his imagination.

More importantly, he was not confused. I am confused. And getting confuseder.

I am getting wonderier about our mental welfare.

Well, you should be if I cannot get up from the bed and recover the wanton emotions of the night. It's very cold outside. I saw this mechanic wearing a pair of overalls into which he had inserted a heating pad and he had plugged himself into a power strip and was working comfortably. We could make rigs such as that.

If we got a generator and put it in a red wagon we could make it to the liquor bunker warmer and making more noise than all the brothers' Buicks combined.

We would never be fucked with hooked up to a generator.

Are you making some roundabout insult?

I am just having a vision of us wired to a loud Honda generator, smiling in our superwarm jumpsuits, and carrying large unbreakable bottles of vodka unmolested through the ghetto. That is all I will confess to.

It is not a bad vision.

It is a happy vision. It is not a vision of a dark place I cannot rescue from abstraction. I am done with all that. This Red Flyer walk in heated suits is a Studio-Becalmed vision, and I am going totally with it.

I want orange electrical cords and orange suits, like jail suits.

That will be our very best protection, if we look to have escaped and are not in a panic to conceal our prison garb.

We will be bad. Unspeakably bad and loud and bold. One of us stays with the generator while the other goes in the store.

Right on.

I can see Studio camped in a pup tent beside Lake Rosa. He gets up at four in the morning under a moon and casts a Dillinger on the lake and catches bass the size of fire hydrants. His uncle remains asleep. There is coffee later, black coffee boiled in a black pot over a fire. An easy morning.

What is a Dillinger?

Torpedo bait, propellers fore and aft, striped like a zebra.

Is this a joke about primitive bass fishing?

Well, it was a funny bait and the fishing was primitive—the bass back then hit anything in the water, as near as I can tell. Water snakes—there were enough of them that they rained from trees into the wooden rowboats.

You are on a full-on nostalgia roll now.

I am. I am about to envision drinking the tangy water from the orange metal tumbler and petting the rogue water moccasin.

Do we have any heating pads?

No.

Jumpsuits?

No.

Metal tumblers?

No.

Dillingers?

No.

&

Did we party last night?

Not, to my knowledge, beyond the usual, the genteel talktail party we always hold. Why?

Because I notice that all the knobs to the stove are off the stove.

They are gone?

No, on the kitchen floor.

Neatly or scattered?

I would say they are in a configuration that is between neat and scattered. As if they fell from the stove behaving like apples falling from the tree are wont to behave: not far.

That is an interesting idea, stove knobs as fruit of the stove.

Well, the fruit is on the ground.

I am without answer.

A stove-knob burglar came in and was frightened off the booty by something?

One of us sleepwalks and likes to pull appliances apart? Were you punished for playing with the stove as a wee?

Did another appliance molest the stove—did the toaster oven pull her knobs off?

Did a bull come into our china shop? I would like to know who coined that conceit, the bull in the china shop, it is not bad at all.

I wonder if a bull has ever actually got into a china shop.

I would think, in the long reach of time, it not unlikely, at least once. A bull running, say, down a street in Spain could easily detour into a fine shop. Remember your laws of thermodynamics. I'll say it was Dickens, Sterne, one of those guys.

I am a little depressed.

I am too.

Nothing novel.

No.

We should reknob the stove.

I'm going to. I left them on the floor only for evidentiary purposes. The crime will not be solved, we might as well sweep up the evidence.

That could be our motto for Life. Life will not be explained; sweep away the evidence.

&

The hindmost hand.

What?

I have had another vision, of "the hindmost hand." As a phrase, not as a thing.

What does it mean?

No idea. But I like it. It comforts me.

It would be possible to take succor from the hindmost hand.

Far superior to that from the foremost hand.

Inarguably.

We have fallen on the right side of the fence on that one, yes.

And how discomforting is the hindmost foot, or the foremost foot, compared to the balm proffered by the hindmost hand?

That foot is not a halcyon idea any way you put it.

No. We favor the hindmost hand.

The hindmost hand helps us, leads us last through the door.

The hindmost hand on the small of the back.

It hands you peace of mind.

It sits you in the shade, the hindmost hand.

It shows you the valley, the light without trouble, the happy shadow.

It calms the water before you.

It hands you the halter to the gentle horse of Life.

It gives you a piece of candy when you thought you were left out.

It spanks you when you need spanking.

It waves a hearty farewell when you are leaving.

The hindmost hand greets you forever.

The hindmost hand helps you over the last hill.

The hindmost hand hauls you into the Final Alps of Heaven.

Studio Becalmed shakes your hand with his hindmost hand.

With your own hindmost hand you say, Hidey, finally, to Studio, and you rest.

Your long sojourn is done.

You may discard your electrified orange jumpsuit.

Let's not go there again.

&

I have lost my mind, I am comfortable with having lost my mind, and I plan on having my mind stay lost.

That is Caesarian, almost. What precipitates this observation?

Por esample: I have spent the better part of the morning cutting up my BVDs for rags, making nice usable little patches of soft polishing cloths by cutting along the seams. This surgery is done as carefully as if it were construction, not dismantling.

This is not irrational behavior. We can be compelled to many enterprises like this. The brain wants order. The soul likes clean lines, man. The isolated "cotton panel" speaks to it.

Yes. But I am saving the elastic waistbands, because they are generally unexhausted elastic, which I cannot throw away.

This too happens: waste not.

Yes. I plan on offering these waistbands to girls.

Whoa now.

Yes. To girls who come over. These old underwear waistbands will be given them and they will put them on as ur-bikinis, or strapless thongs, and be seduced by them.

I see.

I see that you hesitate to subscribe to the plan. There is a place in the plan for the skeptic: for a fee I will let you inhabit a closet and witness the seductions by waistband.

I will get in the closet and hold my breath.

Now you are coming along.

I have old underwear of my own.

Well join us on the outside, then. The scissors are in the proper drawer.

I'm there, dude. I am so there.

I told you that losing the mind is agreeable.

Who would fight it?

No one in his right mind would fight losing his mind.

Extremely well put. That epigram is evidence that our talk is not for naught. We come up with things, here and there.

As would, I think we admit, monkeys at a typewriter, but still, *we type*.

Do you know any girls to call?

No.

We will depend on the drop-in by kind stranger?

Apparently, yes. Unless you know some.

I fear I do not.

I didn't think you did.

All right. I shall dismantle my underpants. I shall whittle them into magical charms. We'll both be ready.

We are prepared. We are loquacious gentlemen with magic lingerie awaiting company. We should have a sideboard of liquor and a man to serve us. We should have important appointments we prefer not to keep. We should have vintage cars well garaged.

We should have a lot that we do not.

We have what we have. We are not to complain.

Complaint is unchristian, untenable, uninteresting, unadvised, undone underwater.

Undone underwater?

Correct. One should not complain underwater. It is less indicated than complaining above water.

And we live, figuratively speaking, if not literally, underwater.

So we do not complain.

We don't.

&

This talk of specious lingerie has had an adverse effect on me.

How so?

I dreamed of a Japanese girl. She walked by me in a sheer peignoir, if that is the term for a short jacket. My bedroom French is not vast. Underneath were the obligatory bra and panties. They were embroidered with a perfect bold black Ottoman design. So that there was the likeness of a sultan's signature on the mons.

What was adverse in this?

It was so striking that as she passed, without regard to me, of course, I was taken by a sigh of resignation, and then I nearly wept. I teared up. I thought of my wife.

You have a wife?

I had a wife.

Oh. Of course. We all had a wife. Wife is a synonym for past.

So I had a vision, inspired by this well-designed and well-positioned embroidery, of my wife in the perfect past, before it . . .

Became the past.

Yes.

And you cried.

I could have. I looked at the girl, who had walked by me and stopped on a gymnasium floor with padding on it for floor routines, and who stood there not thirty feet away still not regarding me, and I could have wept, but at this point I am offended by my sentimentality and getting everything in check, and finding fault with the girl. What is she doing in a serious gymnasium in high-fashion slut gear—you know, that kind of takedown.

Perfectly sensible defense. She looked good.

No. *Delicious*.

I feel your pain, dude.

Really striking underwear, I'm telling you.

&

Where would you like to go?

I would like to go to a place where there are orange fields and sweet young dogs to walk in them with. There is a small wind at all times, large wind at night. Things bud and decay in equilibrium, light and shade play together nicely. If things are named, the names are known but not used overmuch. Forgetting and remembering have shaken hands.

What would you do there?

I would play my little record player, a fabric-covered box for 45s with the fat spindle. I would be alert to birds. I would never hurt anyone's feelings because I would never see anyone.

Would you not work?

Not at more than I have described.

Would you not eat, then?

It is entirely possible that I would not.

Obesity would not present unto you the challenge it presents to most.

No.

All right. I can see this place too. I could come with you.

No. You would need find your own.

I see that that is so. Would you do anything besides play the records and regard the birds?

I would write a book called *The Ways in Which I Have Been a Coward.*

A slim volume or—

No. Exhaustive, and exhausting. It troubles the prospect of my place, with my sweet dogs and old records and crisply singing birds. I might not write it. One more manifestation of the cowardice.

Well, what matter is but one more?

Exactly mine own sentiment. We are so *d'accordo* that if anyone could accompany another to a magic place, you could me.

Yes, and horndog reciprocal, I am sure. But we know better.

We know better.

&

Would you care to go—

I would care to go fishing in that orange light I was telling you about. Some green frondage, in a wind. Either a monkey or a boy who resembles a monkey.

That is all you need.

No. I want also a canteen full of water, a tidy bureau of clothes, a postcard in my bungalow sent to a previous occupant, a lamp, a broom, a skillet, a spider, and a storm.

That is all you need.

That is all I need. Yes.

&

You would wish to be a man?

God no. Why do you ask?

Perhaps I misunderstood a complaint . . .

I do not wish to be a man. What you may have heard was my wondering how it is that I am not one, and do not care. This was at least my position at an earlier date.

It has advanced?

Yes. Now that I have had time to reflect a bit, I see that the situation is really considerably worse. I am not merely not a man. I am not even properly a boy, a good boy. But I have affected the costume of a good boy.

And mien? Is this a place we can finally use that word?

I think so. Or countenance.

So you are not even a boy.

No. I am a coward, an ass, and something else that I had my finger on last night but have now conveniently again forgotten.

Again?

Yes, it is convenient to forget one is a coward and an ass and whatever egregious else one is as frequently, or a little more frequently, than one recalls.

Go get us some coffee. I feel already tired today.

Alas, perfect, you jog me well, you queer musketeer: I am a *lazy* coward and ass.

Were we born lazy or did we through industry of some kind, some noble force, get tired?

That is the hopeful way to look at it, but I fear not. Why dispute it? Why struggle? A coward struggles to not admit he is lazy, or an ass, or a coward. There is bravery in surrender.

If you surrender you are brave and not a coward. I think you are in a jam here. Or is it a jamb?

In a jam of logic or in a door jamb of . . . I'll get the coffee.

&

We have need of adventure. Let us have one.

Summon Studio Becalmed.

From the dead?

The land of adventure if there is one. We will say to him, Studio, we poor cowards and asses are lazy and afraid, can you help us?

And Studio will say?

Fresh from the dead, he will say, Where is Jayne? Where are the Alps of Heaven? Where's my dog? I at least must pet my dog.

Your dog is right here, Studio. We took good care of him. He is about sixty years old but there he is, not a hair on him, and Parkinson's, but he is well drugged, so do not mind all that shaking and drooling, it's the best we can do.

You are a mean bastard.

Who?

You.

Is that you saying that to me or Studio saying that to me?

That, to you, am saying, I. To speak to Studio Becalmed about his dog like that!

Studio is dead now over sixty years; I think he can take care of himself.

It's not exactly the Boy Scouts.

Who said that?

Studio said that.

What the hell does that mean, Studio? "It's not exactly the Boy Scouts"?

I cannot believe the tone you are taking with Studio. He's dead, and he's in our house.

He's our dead houseguest.

Yes, *exactement*.

Where did we go so wrong, Moonpie?

To be speaking this way to the beloved dead?

In the Bakersfield in which we do not have a life, yes.

This, to you, confess, must, I, to not having a clue. But sore wrong we turned, and we are not young girls anymore.

&

I'm just a mouthful of pajama air.

I can't play the accordion.

Picasso could paint.

&

I fell down once and did not get up for ten days.

Where was this?

In France. Or Belgium. Or Switzerland. It's murky over there.

Troppo vino?

Couldn't get enough.

This falling down and not getting up was not vino-related—

No. I fell down, and I could not get up. It was pleasant. I was speaking but no one could hear me. They were concerned for me, in twos and later fives, reaching out to me literally and figuratively. I wound up in a bed. There was no ID, or OD, or MO, or whatever it is called.

Diagnosis?

Yes, there was no inside diagnosis, outside diagnosis, or any known mode of operation for it. I fell down, couldn't get up, and ten days later got up, said thanks, and walked out.

Without paying.

They would not take my money.

This all, I take it, was before I knew you.

Yes.

Because you don't seem to have this kind of purposeful life now, since I have known you.

No, those were the good old days, sho nuff.

Have you ever seen those clips of flamingoes walking in water to a rock 'n' roll sound track and it looks like they are stepping to the beat? Really with-it dancing pink birds?

Yes, I have seen that. Pinking shears.

I like that a lot.

I do too.

&

Are we free?

Insofar as no one is going to pay money to possess us, I deem us free.

Are we free to do anything we want to do?

Insofar as the better of those things cost money to do, I deem us not free.

But we are free to do the free things?

Yes, but we are afraid to do them.

What are we afraid to do?

We are afraid to be men, to engage the world bravely, to be upright in our behavior, to have moral height, to display ditto fiber, to shoot ourselves, to have another dog, to talk to anyone except Studio Becalmed largely because he was not afraid to have another dog and we respect that in another person, especially one safely dead who does not challenge us—

Okay. I get it.

&

I miss my dog more than I miss my parents.

Amenhotep.

Why would one want his dog back more than his parents back?

Because one liked his dog more? Is it a question so difficult that we need a computer geek to configure the answer?

We need them to configure everything else. Why not?

Let me change the subject, though not really: have you looked at yourself well in a mirror recently?

No. Should I?

I do not advise it.

&

Be neat, be brave, be Buster-Brown *bustamente.*

What does that mean?

I do not know. But does it not sound *right*?

It does. I hazard that you are implying that if we'd been neat and brave and Buster-Brown *bustamente* we'd be all right today, instead of . . . this.

That I imply.

I am in the accordion with you. Nice to see that Buster Brown get a piece of the Coppertone girl, wouldn't you say?

You put it more vulgarly than we need to but indeed that is a mythological vision with a purity of force and justice in it.

His hard shiny shoes, his hope, her round unsunned buns, the nippy little dog playing around them.

Her clothes are nearly already off. One can see Buster perhaps struggling to undo the eponymous brogans, comically, sitting on the ground in his short pants, little Miss Coppertone saying, Hurry up, Buster Brown, for God's sake.

Took off a piece of my finger last night in the Benriner. You know there is a cautionary slogan on the slide, WATCH YOUR FINGERS?

I did not know that.

Well, you do now, and I can report that that warning is not bullshit; the bullshit content in WATCH YOUR FINGERS on the mandoline veggie-holder slide thing is one hundred percent not bullshit.

You were brave but you were not neat.

I was as lucky as Buster Brown. Fingernail took the hit. Wicked crescent of ring-finger nail was in the salad, I guess.

I wonder if Howdy Doody ever got laid.

I never had a real grasp on who or what Howdy Doody really was. I see freckles but nothing else—was it animation, a real kid, what? And what exactly did Howdy Doody *do*?

There is a great children's-culture porn waiting to be made in this country.

Go anywhere but Dorothy and the guys. I won't stand for it. The country won't stand for it, bless its heart.

I want to see the Tin Man tell the Scarecrow he's too soft and the Scarecrow tell the Tin Man he's too fucking *hard*.

That I can handle but leave Dorothy out of it.

What about with the exposed Wizard in the basket at the end?

Dorothy never gets in the basket. That's what wakes her up.

We never got in the basket either, my friend, and that is what has us all woke up. We are looking up at the basket.

We is all woke up and nowhere to go.

&

My dog died. He never lost his enthusiasm for me. I now lament that I did not play with him more. It gave him supreme pleasure if I got down on the ground and he would turn me over to go at my face, insanely, insanely wagging happy. I should have spent all day doing this. It was a pure thing, he was unrestrainedly happy. I had the capacity to give something on earth that. There were days, weeks, I did not do this, I schlepped by leaving him alone.

You were a turd, but he knew you were an okay turd, that is why he did the licking.

My father sold his Parker shotgun out of our garage one Saturday morning for twenty dollars instead of giving it to me. I was thirteen or so. Why did he not give it to me? I would like to have gotten to the bottom of that, and to have talked to him and known him at the end. I schlepped right by all that too. But what I am saying is that I regret more not playing with my dog. I think in this preference I am displaying the trait or traits that put us where we are.

Without lives, men who are not neat and brave and Buster-Brown *bustamente,* you mean.

Yes.

Afraid.

Yes.

Nulls.

Yes.

I find that even if I have a coaster to hand I will rarely put my glass on it. I carelessly damage the surface of tables.

This is who we are.

I regard this carelessness carefully. I am industrially idle. This defines me.

There is no point to us.

I will not need another new swimsuit in my time.

We never needed a new swimsuit. We just thought we did.

What do you actually call a swimsuit?

Does one, or does I?

Do you.

I call it a bathing suit.

Would you ever have said trunks?

Never. Sounds preposterous, and I can't say why. My trunks alas are in my trunk.

Once I am in my trunks I will get in the water.

Still, I can hear Jayne say, Studio, put your trunks on, love, let's go for a refreshing dip in the Gulf.

That is the dead speaking, we cannot challenge them. And before they were dead they were neat and brave and not afraid. They can say what they will. I am having a cramp in my gut.

They can say that?

No, I am having a cramp. Now.

You are strange.

Make us a colorful drink with a sugary liqueur. Would you? I feel like a famous lost heroine.

But you are not famous and not a heroine. You are just lost.

Yes, I am comfortable enough. I would like to have a gun.

Not suicide.

Of course not. I would just like some oiled steel, just to behold.

A symbol.

I suppose. Of something. Perhaps not a symbol, but a *thing*.

The old *Ding an sich*!

I think so. We have finally gotten one, one we comprehend.

A good oiled pistol on the table.

To hell with the coasters and where the drinks park themselves, we have oily steel already on the table!

We are making progress.

I did not think that we would, in our time.

&

When I wake up in the mornings the impulse to cry is almost sufficient that I start.

Why do you not, then? As that little imp put it—do you recall this? Throw up right here, Mother.

You are referring to that child in the Sokol gymnasium.

Yes.

That was genuinely funny.

Why was he saying that?

Because she was complaining of having eaten too much spaghetti and said she might be going to be sick.

And they were kneeling on the gym floor.

And the child got tired of her threatening to throw up and tapped his finger on the mat and said, Throw up right here, Mother.

Politely.

Very politely.

No one took any notice.

That is what was so funny.

I recall it now. I am the same woman. I feel like crying.

So do. I will be the same imp. Cry right here.

I am embarrassed at how much weeping I have done in my life, and think that not one more tear is in order, to salvage what I can of . . .

Of what?

That is the question. Just what is this operation about? In

preserving dignity or anything else, what is served? I think I do not quite get it all.

We've been over this.

Yes, and still, and this is what gets me, I feel that I should not cry anymore, even though intellectually, if we should call it that, we know one may as well cry as not if he's as lost as we are.

Lost in the nonwoods.

The closest we are to lost in the woods is lost in the woodwork.

I like it.

Anyway I am unstable until I get the coffee and by jacking my nerves up a bit calm them down.

Is that how it works?

Yes, it's irony, fairly traded and artisan-roasted irony.

Juan Valdez and Joe DiMaggio are taking care of you.

They are the same person except for the kind of women they ran with. They both help me keep on keepin' on. I love that idiocy.

Did Crumb do that? Was it a big Crumb foot marching in the air, leading the fool attached to it?

If it were not Crumb I don't know who it was.

Crumb left us here. He moved to France.

We would too, if we could. We would leave ourselves here.

Why does Crumb get to leave and we don't?

Because we are talking to the dead? Because we are weeping? Because we miss our dogs more than our parents? Because we are the *subject* of Crumb? It's a hard one.

Speaking of *rocket science,* do you recall hearing children of the ghetto proclaim they were going to be *corporate* lawyers? Plain lawyer wasn't enough?

Is that not unlike wanting to be a *brain* surgeon?

Whence this zeal to *specialize* when they are so far in the hole?

Doesn't it mean they know it's fantasy so why not go ahead and make it *sound* fantastic as well? Is it really any worse or different than painting a car June-bug green?

Am I following you?

Can any of us follow Crumb to France? That is what I am talking about. If you cannot, paint your car green or cry all day, it does not matter. Tell people you are going to be a *rocket* scientist when you grow up. They cannot hold it against you. Shoulder to shoulder we look abroad and pray for Crumb to send drawings of feet and thick women.

We know he can because he's eating good cheese.

&

Variegated terrain.

Yes?

I am thinking about it.

What about it?

Is it all it's cracked up to be.

This I trust is not a pun.

No. I think that I am attracted to the idea of variegated terrain, or to the thing itself, and then I wonder what is wrong with a smooth plain—

The sound of wide water! We finally got to use that.

I have never heard that.

Then you are under-read or I am stupid because I think it's Yeats.

Was Yeats a card?

Yes.

Would he have liked variegated terrain or monoterrain?

That is close to monotrain.

Yes it is.

I don't know. All those guys, they drank, they did not want the ground playing any more tricks than it had to. I am thinking they'd go for monoterrain. Your poets with broken noses are unbecoming.

The mail just came.

It is not worth the powder it would take to blow an ant an inch to go get that mail. I knew a jolly woman in Georgia who would say stuff like that. She had terminal psoriasis at the end. Do you recall when you could get letters from girls?

Those were the days in which hormones ran like gurgling brooks in our veins and melted our knees with need.

Yes, those days, and those days are not these days, and that mail contains nothing.

Moreover, I shudder now to realize it is not Yeats but Trouser Snake Eliot who coined the sound of wide water. I apologize. I have rued the day.

Ease up. The day was rued when we came upon it, or when it came upon us, and beheld us marring the horizon, sitting here like unconquerable savages, men missing their dogs and talking pointlessly unless talking to the dead. Let's sharpen something.

Do you recall the Mexicans sharpening the big knives on the concrete abutments under the bridge and cutting up the sharks?

I will never forget it. They were not big knives, they were outright plain old simple all-they-could-get machetes. Slicing up sharks with machetes!

Hand to mouth.

Mouth to hand.

Hand to hand.

Mouth to mouth. They were not bums sitting on their hands and complaining.

We are good at it, being bums. In our way we have made something also of a desperate situation. It is true that we are not carving up monsters of the deep with farm implements, but—

And that guy writing on the sharks with the charcoal.

I am not sure it was charcoal. It might have been a piece of asphalt. From the road.

This is *making do:* cut up the fish with something you find in the field, establish ownership with something you find on the road, and go home to something that is not properly a home, I am sure—

And not a word of complaint. Heroes!

We should go to Mexico and shut the fuck up. It's the least we can do.

That is funny. It is the *most* we can do.

All right. If the least you can do is congruent to the most you can do, is it an argument to do it or to not do it?

This requires more math than I have.

Is the age more mean-spirited than previous ages?

Except for the Middle Ages, as near as I can tell.

Then I think we should do the thing that is the least we can do even if it is congruent to the most we can do. Board this shack up and head out.

The thing I hate about travel the most is not being able to command a space and relax when you have to go to the bathroom.

That is your chief concern?

Yes.

We go, then.

All right.

Good boy.

I am a good boy.

I am too. And Studio. And we are gone.

Do we terminate the mail, cut off the—

No. Do not even lock the door. Turn something over. We will be the suspected victims of Foul Play.

The bus-driving pedophiles got us.

Our play was foul, and it came home to roost. We will be like John Effing Kennedy.

Except no Marilyn, we did not try to do in Castro, nobody knows what happened to *us*—

Yes, and nobody cares.

We are free men.

We were always free, it just took us some time to see it.

Do you feel free?

I feel as free as a green jujube being wedged from its red brothers in the box.

Spring forth, jujube.

Jujube the man!

Studio, Jayne, Jujube One, Jujube Two, ghost dog, gone.

&

What is a concrete abutment?

Something that butts out made of concrete.

Yes. And this the Mexicans sharpened the knives on. But architecturally, what is an abutment, technically?

I do not know. And you know that I do not know. You are indicting me early in the morning.

I am indicting *us*.

Fair enough. We know nothing.

We are innocent of knowledge.

We are innocent period.

Guilty.

We are guilty of being innocent? Do I smell the big Iron?

No, it is not the Iron. Of being innocent is what men like us are most guilty. It is our central guilt. There is no excuse for it. Here: do you have any idea what is meant by one currency weakening against another, or one nation seeking to duplicate its own government in another country by invading it? I am saying, Can you read a newspaper and understand what you are reading?

No.

Because you are innocent. Here's another form of the questions: if you were to sally forth onto variegated terrain and had the option of putting on your Sunday pants, your sunder pants, or your underpants—some song lyrics I think I misheard—which pants would you select?

My underpants.

We are men who find the silliness of that idea attractive. We are innocent. We are guilty.

Of being innocent.

Precisely.

This song said . . . what?

I swear it said, "Put on your Sunday pants and . . ." But it sounded like sunder pants or underpants finally.

It was not sunder pants, that's too archaic and good.

It was not underpants because that does not take itself seriously enough for a million-dollar-making industry-backed recording. Ronnie Van Zant is not going to sing "underpants" dead or alive.

&

Isn't what we are innocent of, beyond not knowing what "weakening currency" means, this: knowing who we are? Of knowing who and what we purport to *be*? Of having a secure sense of our histories and our desires and our—

Yes, we are outside the gravid circle of adults.

We are not burdened by purpose.

We are not even obliged by *point*.

Yet we are here, and from a distance of five yards look not unlike those inside the gravid circle of knowing who they are and what they want.

This is not quite true. I have just seen photos of Chinese telecom executives. They look exactly like Chinese communist big shots from forty years ago. They look like American auto executives, in their posed confidence. We do not look like these men from even a hundred yards. Either they are terrorists or we are terrorists.

Are we what is called "nihilists"?

I do not think so. Nihilists live inside an even graver circle more certain of itself.

Head for that taco stand.

There's grease ahead.

That grease will make it so that you do not give a shit where you take a shit, and shit, my friend, you will.

This I understand. I am an imminent defecator in a land foreign to me.

And this precisely defines us: The others are in a land familiar, at all times, and they are not going to be seized by inopportune bowels. They have a plan for pooping. That is the difference between good CEOs and us.

We are bums, then.

Yes, we are talky bums with decent clothes and odor under control but bums all the same, innocent of survival.

The tacos are a quarter and they are shaved off that cone of meat and flies there onto a piece of wood. We will die.

We certainly will. We are afraid of life but not of death.

Hello.

Hello, good-bye. We must learn to say, Double tortilla, no onions.

Tasty!

&

I'm having a hard time.

Why is that?

I do not know.

I mean, what is the complaint?

The complaint is I am having a hard time and I don't know why.

You are testy today. You know that we believe a man not in the hospital or not in jail is not really having a hard time.

We say we believe this, and superficially we do, but deep down we complain like children.

We need to be beaten then, like children, until we straighten up.

Probably so. Then we could complain about the beating.

It would be a specific and tenable lament, unlike this I-am-having-a-hard-time shit. Just what does your hard time today consist of? Can you put a finger on it? Isn't that a lovely expression?

To put my finger on it, something is percolating in my bowels, my life insurance policy has lapsed because I did not make the payment in time, my tax return is not yet complete, it awaits word from my broker whom I believe I have offended with a joke about his deplorable politics, I await word from a colleague at work whom I have offended by calling a nitwit, a willing young woman is to visit with whom I cannot see having carnal relations, with her is an unwilling one with whom I can, yesterday I did not eat anything, and apparently do not wish to today, though this coffee is nice, thank you; I miss my dog, I am in this foreign country and do not speak, I miss my wife, I live under the constant low roiling purple soft cloud of divorce about ten feet off the ground and tracking a man like a dog with a better nose than the dog I miss had. There. For starters.

I do not see that you have a problem. You just have a whining problem.

This is true. Thank you. I feel better. Much better.

Don't go getting carried away.

No. Do you know the difference, by the way, between France and India?

I do not.

If you look out the window for thirty minutes in France you will see a dog take a shit; in India, a man.

Why would a man capable of or interested in an observation of this caliber think he has a problem?

You have been most helpful to me today, sir.

&

Do you see this hazard of steel appearing—

What is a hazard of steel?

I don't know. But it appears to recede into infinity, rails of steel or a channel of steel, somewhat like a steel trough, except it is heavy and precisely machined—it is like a giant pistol action the size of a railroad, you might say.

All right. Let's say I might say that. It is not clear to me why I am saying it or why you are saying it. What *about* the hazard of steel?

Well, I see it. In my mind.

You see in your mind a railroad-sized pistol action receding out of sight. To the exclusion of all else?

Well, no. I don't see exclusively the hazard of steel all the time, but when I do see it I will say that at that moment I see nothing else. It fills the screen as it were.

So you don't see, say, cedar trees and rabbits marching also into infinity beside the perspective of steel.

No. And that is a good word, *perspective.* It is a perspective and that is what occupies your mind, not the surround, just as in seventh-grade mechanical-drawing class they never had you draw in the parking lot and trees around the building that also I might note seemed poised to recede into space.

So what you have is like a seventh-grade vision of a giant pistol action stretching let us say from New York to Moscow.

Or beyond. The steel looks so polished, so well cut!

Nicely oiled?

Finely oiled!

And when you behold this vision, you are disturbed by it, or—

No! Made completely, utterly content. I love the hazard of steel. I want to work the giant action!

Do you think it tenable that our brains have gone?

Yes I do.

&

Have you had further occasion to view the hazard of steel?

No. It has been replaced by a vision of flowers.

Giant flowers issuing from the giant pistol action?

No. A field of gladiolas. Tended by a blind man. On a three-wheeled ATV. The glads are sold from a jar in a shed by the road on the honor system. The honor system tends to stick in the mind when you see it.

I will never forget seeing a refrigerator full of Orbit beer sold on the honor system at a motel in the Florida Keys. I wish I could recover that moment.

Isn't it wanting to recover moments that undoes us?

Yes, I suppose that is what undoes us.

How should we seek to not wish to recover moments, then?

I propose two ways: repudiate the recovering of moments as childishness and embrace the covering as it were of the present moment in such a way that the recovery of a moment past seems moot.

It would seem to me if we could effect option two that the repudiation of the recovering of past moments as childish would be moot, so you are really proposing one method.

So be it.

It is simply seize the day, in the way that the day was seized the day you saw an Orbit in a rusty refrigerator on a slab in Pine Key at the Rainbow Motel if it was not the Peace Inn and put twenty-five cents in a cup for it and thought you were in an already passing-away time, and were, but you were seizing that time at that time and were in it and now it stands for its very vigor as the kind of moment cleaner and better than the current dull ones you are not so seizing and enjoying.

Yes. That was a mouthful but I think you have it right.

Have you noticed that everything is leaning a little bit today?

Leaning?

Yes, off-plumb. Maybe it is just me.

Are you dizzy?

No, but I swear that pot right there is hanging not vertical, and those decals you pasted up of that grasshopper are not symmetrical anymore, and, you know, isn't everything just a bit *leaning*?

I think you are right.

Should we straighten everything?

I think not. I don't think us capable, one, but I see no reason to undo the charm of things leaning. Things are finally getting in tune with *us*.

About time.

Yes. Leave the horse's mouth alone.

I wish we owned a forklift. Be fun to drive it around and pick impossibly heavy shit up.

&

Is it amazing how fast things break down now?

What things?

Us.

Oh. Yes. But that has, we have, always been breaking down.

That is technically true but when I was twenty and looked like a beautiful girl and beautiful girls would pay attention to me because of it you could not tell I was breaking down.

Well you can tell it now that you look like an old man and will soon look like an old woman.

You are vicious.

Yes. Do you know the original meaning of *vicious*?

No.

Me either, but I recently read it and it is something quite different from what one is when he tells someone he is an old man soon to look like an old woman.

Probably in the early innings of *vicious* there was not enough meanness about for old men to be telling old men they would soon look like old women.

&

I recall it: tending to vice. That's all vicious meant.

Well you don't tend to vice, you are *vicious,* a vicious bastard.

I must say we have much improved the word over time.

As we decline the words get better.

That is how it should be. They are our children.

We become old women and the words go skateboarding.

I am down with it. I need a vicious drink today.

I wish we had a live-in bartender.

We should have an entire Court. We are princes.

Yes we are. Just exiled before our time.

I feel like walking in the woods that do not exist and talking birds into sitting on my hand with the promise that I will not hurt them.

I had a dream that someone's wife visited me in bed.

Anyone's wife?

No, a particular someone whose name I daren't mention. I was dreaming in the dream that I was kissing this woman and woke up still within the dream to discover that I really was kissing her. It developed—in three syllables or fewer—that she had been trying to get me to meet her down at the dock but that my prudence did not allow it so she knew the only way to have me was to slip into bed while I was helpless and asleep and have her way, and this alas she had done, she was as proud and bright as Jack

Horner. She was facedown in the bed at this point and spread her legs and said, Do you like my apple?

Did you avail?

I took a bite of the apple before it occurred to me I was not free to bite with abandon. Husbing.

Ah, you had the old husbing-still-looks-at-his-wife delusion.

Yes. Well, I was after all in a dream state. And this apple was worthy of inspection, which is why I straight off took a bite.

Why can we not live real lives?

I don't know.

&

We are done?

It would appear we are.

I have noticed this morning that my shins have grown thin and sharp.

We have bird brains, why not bird legs?

I suppose. Still, when your leg feels like a knife, it is sad and alarming, quietly.

I can accept that.

I want some bread pudding.

Let us locate the best bread pudding within our reach and get on with dying.

Do you know what *cabildo* means?

No.

&

It's a miracle.

What's a miracle?

Nothing.

Why'd you say something was?

Felt like it. It felt like the time.

You've waked up mindless again?

Yes. Just what is wrong with that?

I have tendered no criticism of mindlessness.

You better not.

I merely seek to verify.

Isn't *something* a miracle, though?

I'm sure something is.

I am too.

I don't see one at hand.

Well, they're rare, that's inarguable. If they were common, they would not be called miracles.

Your logic is sound. It is not altogether mindless.

Coffee bean.

What?

Would not a coffee bean be a miracle?

Easy now.

Why is not a coffee bean a miracle?

Because then, ah, so is a cup of coffee and an idiot, or two, drinking it. Why not say a bird, or for that matter, a bird's *leg*, is a miracle?

Not a wing?

Wing schming. A bird's leg came off a dinosaur for God's sake. A scaled powerful appendage shrunk to one five-hundredth of its original size and attached to an animal that can *fly*. Where would miracles cease if we allow coffee beans and birds' legs? Miracles would not cease. They would never, properly speaking, not begin, never *not have begun*.

Everything is a miracle.

Exactly. And a minute ago you said nothing was a miracle.

A minute ago nothing was. And you said I was mindless.

You were. Now you're not.

I am happy. Are you happy?

No I am not happy.

I wish you were.

I do too. I am happy that you are happy.

If you were happy too, it would be a miracle.

Yes it would. It would it would it would.

Look: here's a coffee bean, a bird's leg, and your happiness. Is it so far-fetched?

You remind me of the halcyon time when my father camped out on Lake Rosa with his strange uncle Jake. I envisioned Studio doing this earlier, but really it was my father. They did this on private land. There were so few people then, and the few people knew each other, so that camping on private land did not then, as it does today, constitute trespass and grounds for prosecution and trouble. They camp out on somebody's land who does not mind and they catch giant bass by throwing the lure called a Dillinger. A Dillinger looks like a small wooden cigar with propellers at each end and it is painted to resemble a zebra. Actually it is painted to resemble a convict suit, black-and-white striped, hence its name. This caught fish in that miraculous day of absent litigation, friendliness among people, and large and plentiful game. I feel like weeping.

I am weeping.

We are fools to even try to be alive now.

We are not, really, alive now.

No, we are not.

We are not miracles either.

No. I can see my young father and this odd fellow Jake having coffee they have brewed over a small fire in one of those agate coffee boilers that look in profile like a laboratory beaker, sort of—

Triangular-shaped.

Exactly. Bad coffee badly brewed, overbrewed, boiled probably, actually ruined-ass coffee that they find delicious, that *is* delicious if you are lying there on that clean ground under the live oaks on the slightly painful acorn caps apprising the morning and the fourteen-pound majestic monsters you have caught on such a ridiculous artifice as the Dillinger, which is at rest suspended from a rod and reel leaned against the live oak they are under. My father will go into World War II as a marine and suffer hardship that is somehow not different from this very pleasure he and Uncle Jake are enjoying now.

I don't see how you make that connection but I do not dispute it.

Dispute nothing.

Disputing nothing is the first step unto miracles.

Disputing nothing is the first step through the difficult door of happiness.

I'd like to find a pill and go back to bed. I'm wore out.

Go on. I'll tidy up and look out the window some. I'm tired too, Helen.

I wish Helen had slept with Tim.

Tim's whole life might have taken a different course if she had. Oh, Tim, I'm tired. I'm tired too, Helen. It was brilliant.

But it did not make her get untired and sleep with him.

She was young.

She was tired.

We are all tired. Who is ever not tired?

I know, but she was young.

&

I have been waked up by one of my stupid nightmares.

There is another kind?

Yes. There are real nightmares that are inventive and psychologically telling and entertaining to recall and that demonstrate all manner of deep-seated truth etc.

That you pay people money to interpret and so forth.

Right.

That you never forget.

Right. These I am talking about you cannot remember for five minutes, if that. They operate just long enough to get you out of bed, which apparently is their purpose.

Give me an example.

Okay. Say you are divorced after a long period of chilly relations and there is no prospect whatsoever of reconciliation. A stupid nightmare would have you envision very sentimental carryings on between you and this estranged wife and imminent desire to get back together develops, and great wistfulness, in fact tearfulness, at such a prospect, and you would wake up crying, gently.

Someone you pay money to might tell you that is psychologically telling etc.

Yes and he would be an idiot. Here's a better example: You are fishing with a fly rod on a dock and hook a very large panfish, monstrously large, trophyesque, and call your serious fishing buddies over to have a look before you release it. They are casual about it because this panfish is not prize game in their view. You somehow wind up at the transom of a running boat with the fish still on, and have to set the rod outside the boat because the fish is hung up and cannot now be properly released, and as you try to climb back over the transom and the outboard motor to free the fish these buddies start the boat forward which will chew up your rod and the fish and quite possibly you once this cartoon develops fully in its improbable way.

These guys are assholes?

Well yes they are but that is not the major import of the action. There are weird pieces of lumber or dockage or trees or something that keep you from freeing your rod and the fish that are so improbable that these guys cannot be faulted for not comprehending the restrictions you are encountering; you cannot actually comprehend them yourself. There's a two-by-four across the rear of the boat that keeps you from stepping out to get your rod which is at the fore of the boat.

They are moving the boat forward *toward* your rod?

Yes, sort of.

How did it get up there?

I know not. It's a dream.

I'll say.

This is what I was telling you: It's a *stupid* dream. It does not make sense, and it does not make the perfect nonsense a real dream makes. It makes only this stupid-ass sense.

You need to quit having these.

That's what I'm talking about.

Is it an expensive rod?

Eight or nine hundred dollars for the rig. The fish is more spectacular than any that is actually alive now or in the past. It will be destroyed.

You don't have to pay me to tell you this but this is a dream born of depression. That's all it is.

So what do I do?

No idea. Stay awake.

Good idea.

A man and all his effects.

What?

I was just having an idea: A man and all his effects . . . is a sad business, you get right down to it. Grave to him, silly to the universe. He can't get rid of the crap that weighs him down. He cherishes his ditty bag. He needs a house fire, of course, but he also needs a mind fire.

&

I want to go to the yard sale up the way.

Do you want more shit?

No.

Then—

I know. But what if there is good shit?

You don't want more shit.

The *last* thing I want is more shit, but what if there's good shit there, and it goes ungotten?

It won't go ungotten, someone else will get—

Get the good shit, simple as that. Hat up. I am having a vision of old monofilament. That is what I most need today.

I hope they have kittens in a box and you get one.

What if they have, like, possums in a box? Free kittens in one box and "Possum's $10" in another? That's what *I'm* talking about! I am talking about acquiring shit no one in his right mind acquires and paying for it and being troubled by it the rest of your life, moving it from house to house, in this case being put in the hospital by it, and so forth. I am talking about *living,* my friend.

I wonder if what you are talking about is the kind of lunacy that inspires a man to run for president, when it's at the other end of the spectrum of affluence.

The man who can't stand for other people to get the good

shit that he doesn't need but must have lest they have, when he already has money?

Yes. The poor kleptos go to yard sales, the rich run for president, out of the same impulse.

Just hat up, de Tocqueville. That fishing line calls me.

&

Was that a . . . what was that?

What?

That flew by.

What flew by?

That is what I am asking.

You are asking what flew by.

Yes.

I saw nothing fly by.

Come on—it was like a condor, blew right through here about six feet high.

Didn't see it.

Dude, you should have *felt* it.

Didn't feel it.

I have a headache.

Take a nap.

&

In the broadest sense of the word: helmet.

What are you talking about?

I have no idea.

Are you insane?

I think so. Isn't that our goal?

I suppose it is.

So: helmet. In the broadest sense. I want to get the pols and the voters together and say, "In the broadest sense of the word, helmet, people. What I am doing here, on the ground, I am a commander on the ground, listen to me, I am thinking outside the helmet here," and so forth, until someone objects—

And you know that no one will object.

Of course no one will object, unless they are told to object. Helmet.

Iyuh hayev ayuh mayarble.

What?

It's my new language: two-cylinder instead of one. Two-stroke.

Liyuk, cayool?

Roieet.

We are insane.

We are inSAYane.

&

Dude.

What?

Nothing.

&

Are we going to have fun today?

No.

Are we going to live today as if it is the last day of our lives?

No.

But we know from the testimonials of Close Callers that we should.

Yes.

But we don't do it.

No.

Why not?

We can't conceive of how you actually do it.

We can't?

No. Go ahead. Propose that we live right now as if this is our last day. What do we do? Where do we go?

I want to sit right here and think about The End.

See? Why don't you ACTUALIZE yourself? Have you been to Tahiti? No? Then you must go. Now. Be gone.

Jesus.

See? You see?

God wasted two whole spaces on us as human integers. We're nils in terms of becoming all that we can become.

Actually, we are negativos, like junkies, except we don't

even have the desire or the drive for self-satisfaction like a good junkie. He has at least his want and he seeks to claim it.

We just don't want. And don't satisfy.

I don't even really get hungry anymore in a good way.

&

We're out there.

We're out where?

There.

We are here. Cornbread are round.

I know. I just feel like saying, We're out there.

The mood is upon ye for nonsense again?

It always is. You know that.

Yes. The stove is the only sane party here.

But, really, doesn't "We're out there" feel just about right, and finally true, and agreeably unpresumptuous—

The smart retarded we go for?

Yes.

I admit that it does. We are out there.

I can barely see it, the there out there. It's deserty but not in a rich, real way—no cacti or lizards or mesa or Santa Fe shit, not even the vast ocean sand roll of the African shtick. Just kind of sand-seeming blah. Like the, well—I just saw one of these—like a Polaroid picture that doesn't develop into anything except some toxic-looking edges and a grayish center you keep hoping will look like something soon but it never does and you put it in a drawer and keep it anyway until your house is so full of crap like it that you pray for a house fire to rid you of it all, and your life in a sense resembles the drawer and the house full of likewise crap around it and you want a fire to clean it up too, and in lieu of that you start longing to be in a gray undeveloped place that is represented by "out there" in your tired brain, and you go around saying, "We are out there"—

When in fact you are not, but you badly want to be, out there—

Exactly. Make us a drink if you will.

I will, my brother. I will go to the porch and make them on the washing machine, which I like to do, and from there I will call into the house and say, "I am out here making drinks," and even this little echo of "out there" will gratify us a bit and keep us from being depressed and terrified.

We are geniuses.

We are not taking the pills that give you the Tantric ejaculation.

Grossoroni. I want clean gin with juniper berries in it. I can see a juniper berry rolling on the Sahara like a BB on a sixteen-lane highway. You remember when that joke was "four-lane" highway?

You remember when we thought the idea of Chernobyl was bad?

I have no idea what a juniper berry actually looks like. I picture a blueberry crossed with a caper. Rolling across a dune as tall as Fate.

As what?

Nothing. I've lost it.

When I make the drinks on the washing machine, there is always a tiny bit of sand on the lid under the glasses and I swirl the liquor and hear a faint gritty noise and it makes my day. At this moment "out there" is precisely under the glass in my hand.

You have lost it too.

No contest.

We must have our desires, even if they are not desires.

Perfect smart retard! We should coin something so objections will abate if we go public—like "smard."

If I had access to a child I would buy it some marbles today. I would please the little bastard with something lovely and love the little bastard for being pleased and being lovely itself, the little bastard I would by that point not be calling a little bastard but would in fact by that point be in love with. My brain has become like unto a dog's, I think.

A dog is smard, very smard.

The essence of smard.

&

What about airplanes?

What about them?

As Out There.

Well . . . yes, but a rather populist view isn't it?

I don't mean the Out There of being out there in one, alone and free and silent and all that horse. I mean the hangar, the clean huge spotless concrete floor. The plane with no grease on it. The brilliant dials and gauges. The firmitude of the wings. The good paint. The spanking new of things or the seasoned worn-glove old of things, nothing shitty. You know, a small plane in a good private hangar. I feel out there just imagining myself next to a plane like this.

We are not going to own such a plane.

No.

So it's an impossible exclusive Out There, for us. The fuckers.

True. Still: red and white cub on that squeaky weird-ass pebble-grained epoxy flooring, man.

That floor that has like Pollock in it?

Yes.

That is Out There.

For us, though, we are going to be in a field of used Huggies. The Wal-Mart parking lot at noon for us. There we are, dazed from trying to figure out if the bananas are plastic or real.

&

So we are agreed that the best thing would be to be out there on the desert in a clean Piper Cub in the good worn leather seat fingering the rich knobbery.

Assolutamente.

It is dark today.

Looks like hurricane.

Can't be.

I know.

We need a child.

I know. But we won't pass the adoption profile.

Maybe in Kenya we would.

Where the qualification is Mzungu?

I would not think it more demanding than that.

I don't know—the Brits leave their footprint. Could be a pedophile-quotient assay right up front.

So what will we do with this child, assuming we are not proven pedophiles, or if the Kenyans do not care that we are if we are?

I want him to grow to be strong and reserved and smart and take this chainsaw here, which I haven't yet purchased for him, and slowly cut this house apart and burn it for warmth until we and it and everything else in it is gone, and he then, the child, is a stunning athlete and goes to Harvard and speaks well of his two Mzungu uncles whom he could not have done it all without, and he has one of those impossibly beautiful sets of brilliant white teeth and smiles a lot while saying this about us, and we are rotting happily in the sand out there by the little twisted clean Piper Cub wreck in the sand. That is all I want.

Will he not be sad?

He will not.

Why not?

I don't know.

Su visión es mi visión.

For me it comes down to this: We were not sane men, but we were better than many. Our boy will somehow know this. It will sustain him. He conquers the NFL and then Harvard Medical and he knows that he was put there by two old pops who had nothing, least of all pretension. Out of our agreeable daft arises his untaught heroic. That which we so lacked. That is what I want.

What's his name?

Stanley. They have named him Stanley and we want to change it but, agreeably daft, we can't.

Okay. God am I tired.

I'm tired too, Helen.

What?

Nothing.

&

Do you see a problem with my outfit?

Have you lost your mind?

No. I just thought that was funny.

It is.

Do you recall when we wanted to go to the liquor store in the orange jumpsuit with an electrical cord trailing out of it all the way back to the house?

Vaguely.

I recall that we thought of this, and that it was funny or had some point, but now I don't know what the point was, or the humor, exactly.

&

We need things. Let me rephrase that: we need *things*.

I got the first one but not the second.

Things would give us some distraction.

Bass boat, bearer bonds—that kind of thing?

Well, I am thinking, yes.

I thought we wanted house fire.

We do, but I think we want house fire only because we don't have good things that really provide the distraction we need.

Wives, jobs?

Yes. Maybe.

All the things that the people we despise have that we see make them despair, we don't have, and now we want them?

Well, maybe. All we do is talk and sit here. We have nothing. Those people are humanly realized and all that, and I grant you many are fucked up, but cannot there be a few who actually do have it going on? Like, real and smart days, and fun and accomplishments—you have to admit we do not effect that, sitting here doing our thing. Pondering plane wrecks in the desert as a *good* thing.

I heard about this football coach fired twice in the same year by different teams.

Well yes and what about being one that would, say, win the national title twice in three years, have a wife, and children not arrested for anything, have his organization like a little military under him, redeem some criminals by giving them some legal violence to channel their evil intent through, lovely second home like on the beach to keep you from wanting to burn down the primary—don't you think that might be all right, if you could get it?

You are talking about being a real man.

I am.

You will be on medication and having retrograde ejaculations before the week is out you keep this up.

&

I need a saddle pommel. To steer me through the house. Not a horse or a saddle.

Just a disembodied pommel?

Exactly.

We could get you one of those four-wheel walkers and put a set of longhorns on it. You couldn't go through a doorway but you'd be stylin', stuck there.

I just need the invisible saddle pommel to hold on to. I think it's what the rappers are doing when they hold the crotch.

Is your hand going to be out in front of you as if you are riding a saddle and holding the pommel?

No. This saddle pommel is in my mind, and I need it.

I need a shovel to lean on, in my mind only. Also I need to shave the hair off the back of my neck.

That is another kind of want. Unless you purport to do that too with the shovel.

I know it. I don't.

I wish the masseuse team would get here, speaking of it.

Put on the jumpsuit and go to the liquor store.

Not without my pommel. I can't.

Did you hear about the kid who punched out the school-bus driver?

Did he suspect him of pederasty?

That was not intimated in the news report. What was intimated was that an innocent man was attacked by an early irrigible thug.

By what?

Incorrigible.

You said irrigible?

I did.

What does that mean?

I don't know, I've never heard it.

It sounds like it should be a word, though.

It does.

The irrigible thug. Almost the opposite of the incorrigible thug. Is corrigible a word?

I think not.

Then the word for what we mean by corrigible should be irrigible.

Irrigable almost works too.

That *is* a word.

Scrabble master! Give me the jumpsuit and the cord. Plug me in. I'll get Nordic Blue vodka and be a dandy there and back.

I'll hold my pommel if the brothers mess with me. I'll say I'm looking for that irrigible punk that slapped the pederast bus driver and that I aim to seduce him with my suit and my juice.

There is a fine line between humor and stupidity.

The line is finer all the time.

The bird doesn't change.

The bird does not change.

&

Be all that you can be.

Talking bout.

Hongry jack.

Pluperfect.

Tell me a story, Susie Q.

Release me and let me love again.

You never loved.

That is true.

Nor I.

Why is it?

Why are we deformed?

We do not know. Can the deformed see their deformity?

The club foot yes, the club heart no.

Tender is the meat.

I loved the name and the actual thing called the trundle bed as a child.

I made beds with my mother. She taught me the pillow-case thing where you hold the pillow with your chin. It fascinated me for some reason, not knowing immediately why she had bowed her head like that.

What about that weird inversion method, the inside-out grabbing of the corners of the pillow—

No, that is perverse. I won't have it. That is like sock bunchers. Socks should be pulled on I don't care if it stretches the shit out of them, not rolled on like a rubber or something, a rubber on your foot, I won't have it.

There is a lot we won't have.

There is a lot we don't have.

And that by God is the way God wants it. Let's shut the fuck up and not pray.

Tang. What a drink that was.

Do you recall Fizzies?

That was a pioneer, a harbinger of fast-food badness, headed our way.

Is it tenable that our bad appetites are what is actually ruining the world?

Whoever controls the sugar in its cheapest form will control the world. Fifty-five gallons of corn syrup can do more to move and control people than fifty-five fifty-five-gallon drums of oil. The oil can be all gone and people will be fighting over sugar.

You've gone all pundit on me here.

Pundit. Pundit. Pundit. How much pun could a pundit pun if a pundit could pun pun?

Give me the suit. I am headed for the store. The days of the professional drinker are over but we air not whupped yit.

&

We are perfect.

Pluperfect.

Pretorian guards of the sane.

I wish dinosaurs had made it.

No shit.

Don't criticize me. Did you hear that hot rod or whatever the fuck that was last night? What was that?

Loud machine.

No shit.

We talking in circles, we hear where we coming from, but we talking in circles.

I hope my deodorant does not fail.

How long before we smell like old men?

Last year, dude.

Probably so.

Have you seen a lot of chicks coming through here?

Well, it's not the Manson ranch, I'll grant you that.

Do we not fantasize about having the Filipino houseboy to make the drinks?

We do?

I do.

You don't want him for anything other than the drinks, though?

Maybe run the vacuum a little. What would that hurt?

That would not hurt a thing.

I love Lucy.

What?

That was a bizarre and seductive thing to name a show. I do love Lucy.

Lucy who?

Lucille Ball.

Who does not?

People don't actually *look* at her since they were told to laugh at her. She was hotter than—

Yes, it is a widely unknown known fact.

The Widely Unknown Known. I want a show called that. Why don't we storm Hollywood with our genius?

I don't know.

Do you know that the destruction of animal habitat, say that of the gopher tortoise, is now largely in the hands of licensed professionals? That there is so little natural habitat left that the predation of it is reserved to the nonprofit profiteers instead of the real profiteers?

That makes sense but I confess I was not aware of it.

The government of India for example shoots the tigers now.

Is Sunday school still a going thing?

Say what?

It must be, to some extent, but I hardly see how.

Look, if people can be taught still to think "socialized medicine" is the worst thing that can happen, particularly the ones already on Medicare and Social Security, they still make their kids go to Sunday school. Don't you let the BB of your brain roll too far down the razor-blade highway without realizing that.

You're on fire, dude.

If I could I would get up right now and watch Jack LaLanne and exercise with him.

Do you think when we put on the jumpsuit and head for the liquor store we are perversely channeling Jack LaLanne?

When the brothers contest our passage we'll *wish* we were.

I have never seen anything like those fingertip pushups. They don't even do that in cartoons.

Okay, look. Take Lucille Ball and Jack LaLanne. Throw in Barney Fife. Is it not the case that things were once richly conceived and executed by authentically talented people and that today we are pale not even imitators but just goofballs somehow making money going through the motions?

Cancel the subscription!

When I take that multivitamin without eating something I feel a little upchucky.

&

God I feel small and dumb.

Anything happen?

No, the usual small and dumb.

When, what I want to know, did we feel otherwise?

When we were five.

When we *were* small and dumb.

Yes, then we did not feel small and dumb.

Were we large and smart?

I would say we were expansive and hopeful, full of cheer and possibility—we were then the way one is supposed to be as an actualizing human adult, who is actually small and dumb.

It's almost a kind of Darwinian irony, isn't it?

I have no idea what a Darwinian irony is, but I think you have struck the nail on the head anyway.

That is so gratifying, as opposed to striking the thumb.

Or missing the nail.

What is that called, when you miss and hit the wood and leave the impression of the hammer face in the wood?

That is called a . . .

Like, a rose, a . . .

We are senile. Look, here's one right here in the window-sill.

I'm calling it a rosedale.

It is not a rosedale.

I know it is not a rosedale. I am senile, not retarded.

You are small and dumb. We are small and dumb.

Eggzackly. We have proved our point.

&

You know that thing where you are supposed to live every day as if it's your last?

Yes.

Do you have any idea how that is actually done?

No, not beyond that we don't do it.

I know we do not do it. But were we to do it, what would we do?

I have no idea. I sense we have talked about this before.

It frequently troubles me.

Okay. Let's do it. Live every day of our lives as if it's the last day of our life. Let's see, that's LEDOOLAIITLDOOL. It sounds like a Mayan god.

Get me a ticket to Tahiti!

I want to live on the Left Bank! Speak French well!

Paul Newman!

What?

Fucker in a race car drinking beer and not getting fat, every day of his life like the last, ledoolaiitldool! And handsome as shit! So handsome he did not even run around with women!

I want to put my own shoes, or someone else's come to think of it, in an advancing tide of lava!

Ivory-billed woodpecker! Get me to that swamp!

Dancing classes in the afternoon!

That's expensive.

Yes, but.

True. Ledoolaiitldool, how quickly one can forget. Sitting here on a budget. In fact, it's living every day of your life as if it's your last *dime*. That's what it really is.

I saw on TV last night that Jack Nicklaus has three grass tennis courts at his house. Different kinds of grass.

We do not have any grass in the *yard*. The yard is ten by ten feet.

Jack can ledoolaiitldool, we can't—

No, that is not true. That is the conventional failure everyone makes. We can ledoolaiitldool, even without resources, if we can figure out what it really means to ledoolaiitldool. It does not involve going to Paris if you cannot go to Paris. It must involve doing what one can do.

Is there a way of going to the liquor store as if it's the last trip?

What if it is not a matter of doing something but of thinking something?

Hmmm. Rad. It probably is. That is why we can't do it.

We cannot conceive of life as ending today and therefore of living today as if there is no tomorrow.

We would not think that way if we were playing tennis on that court over there and let's say you said, Jack, fuck court No.1, this Bahia shit, I want to be on that clipped Scottish pubic hirsuteness you got over there, thanks for having us out, Jack!

You have lost it again.

I know it. I like losing it.

It may be what we do toward ledoolaiitldool. Lose it.

Lose it like there's no tomorrow.

LILTNT. Liltnt. Lil' TNT.

Here we are at Alfred Nobel!

Einstein!

What?

Well, he won it, didn't he?

I suppose. The nuclear-bomb man got the dynamite man's prize.

How did Nobel get so much money for gunpowder and Einstein so little for so much more?

Conundrum of the age, if you ask me. Teaching at Princeton, an old man.

Is it because the age of colonialism was over so Einstein had only people to blow up instead of people to put to work?

Suits me. Ledoolaiitldool!

Lil' TNT.

&

When was the last time you had a friend?

I do not know.

When was the last time you read a newspaper?

Same answer. Is it the same question?

It is the same question.

Well, certainly it is the same answer.

Did we leave the earth, or were we never on it?

We tried to be on it.

Precisely. You had some friends as a child did you not? Wasn't there a point you even subscribed to a newspaper and thought you were in the game? And then at a point you had no friends and no use for the paper, like a worm in a bed of worms.

Like a what?

Worm bed. The conceit is somewhat forced.

I'd say errant altogether.

Maybe that too. Does it matter? Can a conceit describing a man with no friends and no newspaper be aught but errant? Isn't errancy the issue? Isn't then the errant conceit perfect? Isn't the unerrant conceit to suggest the ultimately errant state—

I get it. My objection to worm bed is withdrawn.

I would not wish to work—not that I wish to work for anyone—for the New Orleans Police Department.

Yeah. Count me out too.

Counting you out too.

NOPD, *unh*-uh.

Would like to take a drive in an old heavy Cadillac convertible on like US 90 somewhere, maybe on a dapply part in a sunny swamp. Purchase something nice for a little girl, put it on the seat beside me, and ride home with it like Clyde Barrow chewing gum and with hair tonic in my shiny shiny hair.

You have lost it again.

Beginning to really like losing it.

&

Sometimes . . .

Yes. That says it all.

I wish it would rain.

I wish I had Kathy to talk into taking her clothes off in the playhouse and then when she tells me her father told her not to do that anymore I could run and hide and be afraid of his coming to my house and effecting the end of me. What if, I wonder, we could know even then that our parents would laugh at something like that, and we could have lived lives of relative cheer and comfort instead of in stupid little recesses of complete ignorance? What I am saying—am I saying this?—is that one's whole life is not having the wit to not be afraid of Kathy's father. This is why we do not know, have a clue, really, how to live today as if it's the last day of our lives. We think we have the score because we can see that fifty years ago we did not have the score, bolting from the playhouse, but the fact is we are bolting from another playhouse today. We do not even recognize it as a playhouse.

You sound like William Faulkner.

Mr. Bill? Why thank you.

&

So, look.

Where?

No, here. At some point we cannot keep sitting here proposing absurdist trips to the liquor store, pondering pederasts on the school bus. Adopting impossibly sweet boys from Kenya.

I want a houseboy until he is Herschel Walker.

I do too. So we keep on with this blather, the want of testosterone, others knowing how to live but not us, and finally there is one of us can't walk or something, do you realize that this can get ugly, as they say?

We enter assisted-living facilities!

No, we don't, but if we do, we still then get transferred to the drool-circle facility. We are in assisted living right now.

So what are you saying?

I think there is a point after which the jokes stop and we have to figure out how to die.

Weeping bitterly and unchallenged by the roadside.

Precisely.

Where does that come from, anyway?

I do not know. I thought it was yours.

Let's say Shelley.

Do you know him?

No.

How did Byron die?

Don't know. Lot of those guys got off with consumption early.

Do you think we could have a duel?

We could joke about a duel for weeks and never do it. What would be the odds of two fatal shots? One of us would be dead, the other unable to off himself, and be charged with murder.

What if one of us has a stroke and the other has to cope?

I dig where you coming from. I need a drink. What about an adventure that wipes us out? Imprudently film the griz.

What?

Film the griz.

You have lost your mind.

It works. You live in a school bus for a few months, talk to the griz a few years, show them off to your waitress girlfriends, finally talk to the wrong griz, and you're out.

I see no griz.

Point.

Is it going to rain?

I hope so.

If it rains my spirits will lift.

&

I like to watch the action glow.

How does the action glow? What action?

No, *glow* is not a verb.

What is *glow*?

Glow is a noun.

I thought *action* was a noun.

No. *Action* is an adjective. Action glow. The glow of the action.

You like to watch it?

Yes, I like to watch the action glow.

What does that mean?

Don't know.

Are you looking at the freeway? A field of lightning bugs?

No idea what I mean.

I distrust people who call them fireflies.

I remember that. Those people. They are the same people would pronounce the *t* in *often* and say *interest* with three syllables. Where do they come from?

They come from a strange room.

Can they be forgiven calling lightning bugs fireflies now that we have killed off the lightning bugs?

Do you recall the occasional accident when a lightning bug got crushed and smeared and the smear glowed?

Yes.

Was that action glow?

I think it was. That is not what I had in mind when I said it but now I think I can say that is what I had in mind, like that. Not restricted to that, mind you.

Of course.

It's a useful concept.

Apparently.

It's not much different, grammatically, from, say, blowhole.

I imagine a whale watcher watches the action glow above the blowhole, in certain light.

That phosphorescent glow in the water, in surf, is that animals of some sort? Is that a smearing as it were of lightning bugs, real small ones, in the ocean?

Either that or it's some kind of elemental sparking.

What, like tiny *flint*?

Am I Jacques Cousteau?

Weep for Phiweep.

He died on a wocky outcwopping.

We are going to hell.

To watch the action glow. We'll enjoy it.

&

Let's run over there and pick that trash up.

That the brothers' trash.

It's in our world, dude, and it's not rocking our world.

It seems to me that the debate about civilization and the nuanced forms it can take, whether democracy is the summum bonum and so forth, whether socialism is tenable or evil, and so forth—

Yes?

Well, the debate can stop as soon as you recognize that a good half the people on earth are willing to unwrap their Snickers and drop the wrapper as they bite into the candy bar. The egalitarian saviors standing next to them can shut the fuck up right then and there.

That is an indelicate and unattractive figure of speech, shut the fuck up.

I find it indispensable in certain instances, this being one.

What if I were to contend that the egalitarian savior who won't shut the fuck up is, though, in a sense dropping his own Snickers wrappers all over the environment as well. They are spewing forth in a self-appointed proselytizing that the simple candy eaters did not ask for.

You are strengthening my case, not weakening it.

I can see that.

Half the world is an animal and the other half a meddling

high-minded egghead and they are not coming together except in certain forms of predation and exploitation of the other. This is why tyrants have their spectacular runs. They force peace momentarily. Then the candy eaters start to get a leg up, or the meddlers do, and the pseudo-truce starts to fray, and someone offs the tyrant, or he dies naturally if he was really good, and it's back to chaos.

So you do not want to go pick up the trash?

I don't, but I would like it not to be there.

Let's just pick it up.

People will drop more of it as we do it. At our feet.

Yes, we will appreciate that as a confirmation of our intellectual superiority. We knew that would happen. We will look around for a Stalin to materialize and stop it. People do not care what is done to them if they see the shit slapped out of the other half.

If you had a good clear fingerprint on a Tayto bag and you could take it to Stalin and get the owner of the print hung, would you do it?

I would do it. I would also gas anyone yelling "In the hole!" at a golf tournament. The people who yell this from the tee would drop dead right there, at the tee. The people saying it near the green, where it is tenable that the ball go in, could be buried to their necks in the sand traps and left there to keep saying "In the hole" until they expired. There would be hundreds of tired decomposing faces in the sand, posing a new kind of hazard for golfer and spectator alike.

All right. While we are at it, I want anyone using a cell phone in a car to be put into a Final Demolition Derby wherein your car has to be moving as a salvation number flashes among hundreds of false salvation numbers flashing from hundreds of sites in the arena, on the walls, on billboards, on the license plates of other cars, on the radio dials inside the cars, and you have to dial these numbers as you drive in the demolition and get the one right number to be saved. Otherwise you drive and you dial and you crash until you die there doing just that.

I think many of those people will enjoy that.

You are probably right. Still, it will be better than the gladiators were to Rome.

&

Do you remember that nice little ham we got?

We got a ham?

Not recently. That girl who is a cook sent it to us.

Like, a real ham?

Yes.

Vaguely.

It was not the standard name but it was the real deal. Like Edwards. An Edwards ham.

That does not sound correct, Edward's ham.

No, but it was a correct ham.

I would like to have some drugs.

I would too, but I am trying to think of the name of the ham.

What you are supposed to do in this instance is save the packaging. A ham of this sort, if I have it right, comes in a fetching muslin bag with a lot of logoage and ethos printed on it. You take the ham out of the bag and put it in the bathtub or whatever other ritual you are so traditionally expected to so fondly perform, perhaps as instructed to do even on this very bag, and eventually eat the ham and discard the bathwater but you save the bag.

Logoage.

Yes, sometimes a want of logoage. Like, just a name, so simple that it *looks* like a logo. "Edwards Ham" might be just this sort of nonlogo logo. Only the cognoscenti know about Edwards Ham, the nonlogo says.

All right. Help me find the quiet Edwards Ham bag.

All right. Maybe we will locate drugs in the search.

Glory be to God.

Lay me down to sleep beside the calm waters. No sheep. I don't want to be on the ground near sheep. Frankly I'd be less bothered if I were on the ground near lions than were I on the ground near things grazing.

Do you have any idea where the ham bag would be?

No.

&

Have you been there when the famous fall down drunk and you must help them up and they get angry with you for it?

We have all been there for that.

When we fall down ourselves and have to help our own self up others get angry with us for it.

Yes. We are the small not famous with whom everyone is allowed to be angry.

When we fall down and get up we can even be angry with ourselves.

Yes.

We are the unthanked, the angry-with.

We are the small.

May we quit?

Quit what?

Quit. As in Thou shall not quit, commandment eleven I guess.

Oh yes, we may quit.

We may be *quitters*?

Oh yes.

People will then be more angry—

Beyond angry.

I think about the slaughter of the Indians. Had we been able to quit, we might not have done that. But we could not quit.

Is that a pink poodle?

I would say apricot.

Is that a cat with it?

I believe that to be a blue creme.

A woman is walking a dog and a cat by our house in these rude suburbs and the dog is pink and the cat is blue. She does not appear to be drunk. Or famous.

She is motoring along. Apricot and blue creme.

Call out to her.

And say what?

I don't know.

No.

Why not?

I am afraid to.

&

Would you be interested in a book entitled *The Cragiator Turns His Boys*?

I suppose I would. What is the Cragiator?

I don't know.

You don't know this book?

This book does not even exist. I have envisioned it.

Well what is the Cragiator?

I think the Cragiator is a fellow named Craig whom his boys call the Cragiator.

His little posse.

Yes, I suppose.

This all makes sense. I recall Studio Becalmed.

I think the Cragiator is of a substantially later generation.

We can bank on it. He cannot be as robust as Studio.

He will be to a degree more pitiful.

Well, easy now, he is after all adolescent, not fully formed. He is not to ride around wanting Jayne Mansfield—

No, you are right, he rides around wanting J Lo. It is the same thing.

Who *is* J Lo?

A pop star. That is a contraction of her name.

When you say pop star, isn't there a specific field of endeavor that one first—

Yes, but they get a little notice in one thing and then immediately are everything and it's just easier to consider them pop stars. I have no idea what J Lo was at first. The Cragiator wants her, man, leave it at that, will you?

I am interested only in the Cragiator's turning his boys. I just hope to God that is not genital in its import.

&

It doesn't matter that it doesn't matter.

What doesn't matter?

I guess I am saying that nothing matters.

I have no idea what you are saying, but when you say "it doesn't matter" what is the antecedent to "it"?

I don't know. It doesn't matter. If it doesn't matter, it doesn't matter what the antecedent to it is.

You have lost your mind.

Yes, and it doesn't matter.

Nothing matters.

Correct.

If elephants go extinct, it doesn't matter.

Technically, no. I admit it is a shame. But a shame does not matter.

If the Hutus slaughter the Hittites, it does not matter.

No. Not Hitler, not Huns.

Ants?

They do not matter.

If buzzards stop eating the dead?

It will smell, the smell does not matter.

If the globe becomes a desert?

No.

If the people who support classical music stop supporting it and it too goes extinct?

No.

If Sears fails?

Well, that matters.

What if you brew a roach with the coffee, as I did not too long ago, the roach sitting like a king on the throne of the funnel into the pot, if kings can be imagined boiled alive on their thrones?

He was sitting there, dead?

He was sitting there, upright, dead, and looking not unhappy.

I think that mattered. I think you could not probably have drunk that coffee.

I did not, after two sips.

It matters if you brew a roach in your coffee then, but nothing else matters.

You sound like a child.

That slur is fully merited. It doesn't matter.

But this idea that "it doesn't matter that it doesn't matter"—this is a different debate.

Yes, it's where I began. Sounding like a child.

No, a child says nothing matters, but it takes an adult to say it doesn't matter that nothing matters, because it may well be that a lot depends on one's claiming that nothing matters. I suspect that, if one makes the claim at all, he is saying that something matters.

Well, the fact is, to say "it doesn't matter that it doesn't matter" is not to say "nothing matters" at all. I said that that was an equivalent position, but that was loose. One does need to know what is referred to by the second "it doesn't matter." As you properly noted.

We need a philosopher here to take over for me. Where's the jumpsuit? I am making a run.

&

You be the Cragiator and I'll be Studio Becalmed and let's go into them hills.

All right as long as I don't have to get out of this chair.

Fair enough. Mount your pony, Sarge. Over in them hills we will have a nice camp.

It will have a canvas water bag hanging by the stream.

I want a pot of beans. Underground beans. What are those beans in Maine that look like cows?

Got me there. I want a hammock and a rifle.

Indian servant ladies.

What?

Indian servant ladies.

I have never seen "Indian ladies" in a phrase. I have never seen "servant ladies" in a phrase. It's like butler Huns, or something.

Well, I'll not say squaws. I don't want squaws. I want a helpmeet with dark skin to tend the beans, that is all, in this heavenly camp we can be in without getting out of these chairs.

I want a Campeche chair, in the camp.

You know Peter Patout's Campeche chair worth a half million dollars was stolen in New Orleans and he got it back?

I do know that.

I had the GERD all last night.

I want a breeze in the camp. The leaves to blow into the stream and flash the silver undersides of the cottonwood, and the

Indian servant ladies' hair to move beautifully in the sun, and the flannel shirts to be the right shirts to be wearing in the wind, and a new-car smell in the camp without a new car in the camp.

I am tired.

I'm tired too, Helen.

I wish Helen hadn't been tired.

She wasn't tired.

I know. Don't be insensitive.

I am too tired to any longer not be insensitive. It takes a lot of energy to be sensitive.

That may be the lesson of civilization.

&

The lesson of civilization is that sooner or later we will fuck everything up, is it not?

Roll tide.

I'd like to get worked up about that, since it's useless to get worked up about that.

Tecumseh was a chief, and Mr. and Mrs. Sherman named their blue-eyed baby boy Tecumseh, and after wiping out Georgia single-handedly without finding any Indians in his path he went out West and found some Indians to wipe out. William Tecumseh Sherman. Doesn't that just chap some ass?

When did you become Wounded Knee?

I am large, in the spirit.

I want a newspaper but I don't really want to read it.

We might want to wrap fish or something, litter box.

It's Friday, someone should suit up get a paper and some liquor and we'd be all set.

I was in a house trailer one time, part of a party of drunks visiting another party of drunks, and the trailer hosts were called Bill and Dick and I was there partying for a good while before I realized that Bill was a woman. She was thin and had curly hair like a Marx brother, and was quiet, maybe I am thinking of Harpo—which one had the angelic white hair? And this Bill leaned forward to get a drink off the coffee table and her shirt opened a bit and I saw tiny wizened breasts and as a result started paying more attention and it developed that her name was Billie Mae or something like that and they just called her Bill. Theretofore I had been desperate trying to figure out if the rust stains on Dick's T-shirt were rust or shit.

You were partying, dude.

Indeed I was.

I have never heard *wizened* used before in speech.

I have never used it before. It is the right word, I think. Her hair was not white, it was very soft-looking and curly, maybe Harpo is not the one I want, which one had brown hair? I had been sitting there trying to figure out how this effeminate queer was accepted by these trailer drunks this way when this whole Billie Mae revelation exploded on me, and these poor little tits, and the shitty shirt everyone was comfortable with, and realizing then that this Dick dude in the shitty shirt was wont to mount little Bill with her curls and little titties.

Frightening. You were having a hardcore intro to boozing.

I was.

It has stood you in good stead.

It made me Army strong. It made me be all I could be.

&

Take me down to funky town if ever you were going to. Dude.

Tell me about it.

I've about had it.

Me too.

I'm done.

The battle is over.

Not lost, or won, but over.

Amen. Take me to funky town.

Can't you see that, at the gates, or there waiting for Charon to tie up and watching that dog closely—is Cerberus on the boat, by the way?—saying, "Take me down to Funky Town, my man."

I 'magine he has heard some interesting disclaimers and directives.

Would I be naive though in thinking that "Take me down to Funky Town" might be a first?

I'd risk it.

What about "I missed you, Charon, you poo poo train."

Bold.

&

After the main thrust of an activity or a venture, should one continue to give it ghost thrusts?

As a dog does?

I suppose.

Well, the air thrust is funny, so I suppose one should do it if one is prepared to look like a dog humping air. For the comedic benefit it confers.

But the ghost thrust is otherwise worthless, you think? Not likely to sire anything?

What enterprise do you have in mind?

Well, I was thinking of us. Sitting here. I think we have asserted ourselves and that now maybe we are ghost thrusting.

We hardly asserted ourselves.

Of course. But we had our say.

We had our say.

What is left? For someone—one's daughter is the most acute vision—to come in and see our effects, our toys, books, how many or few shoes we had, observe how worn or not worn or pitiful they are (in my old man's case it was about nine or seven pairs of Hush Puppies identical except in their pastel colors), put it all in boxes, locate the will, call some people. Feel sad. Go on her way.

Doesn't it seem that there used to be more to it?

How so?

Maybe, more *to people*? So that a passing had a larger moment?

I suppose even now there is the occasional grandee. You saw Kennedy.

I mean on a private plane, though.

I know what you mean.

You, for example, you even wrote some of the books this daughter will handle. What is she to do with them?

She should put them with the others and be done and they be gone. I was a sad sack, end of chapter. I like that. I'd like a drink.

I would too. We can at least not be maudlin on top of everything else.

Let's air hump to the store and repair our spirits.

My little red shorts is already down.

&

We are not yet dead.

Not yet.

At some point we will stop joking about it and become afraid.

We do not have the inner resources that would allow us not to be afraid.

Nor the wit to say that we are in the antechamber to heaven.

We will be in the wheelchair circle, where we said we would never be.

That expression where the mouth is frozen open—is that what is called a "rictus"? Is that Latin? Does it refer to that expression only after death? What is it called when one is in the wheelchair circle still alive enough to drool?

Dude. Slow down.

I was getting worked up.

I could tell.

My Latin was now like sixty years ago. Caesar did not do rictus.

Caesar got out neatly before the wheelchair circle.

I cannot see older civilizations having had wheelchair circles, somehow. What did they do with the old folks too afraid to die?

They stoned them. They never let them collect in corrals, high-profit corrals that offer dignity.

We really are going to be afraid and we really are going to also refuse to die and we will give away the free dignity and purchase the other expensive dignity. I have known this since I could not even put my dog down. Fortunately he was eaten a little bit by a cougar.

That was a stroke of luck.

You are telling me.